To merica

with Thanks

Sometimes

in Dreams

G.L. Helm

[signature]

Sirens Call Publications

Sometimes in Dreams

First Print Edition

Edited by Gloria Bobrowicz

ISBN-13: 978-0615853048 (Sirens Call Publications)
ISBN-10: 0615853048

Sometimes in Dreams

"Whoever loved that loved not at first sight?"
Christopher Marlowe from *Hero and Leander*

"In the combat between wisdom and feeling wisdom never wins. I have told your certain future, my Lord, but knowing will not change it by a hair. When the time comes, your feeling will conduct you to your fate."
Merlin to Arthur in *The Acts Of King Arthur And His Noble Knights* as translated from the *Winchester Manuscript of Thomas Malory* by John Steinbeck

I

The haze at the edges of his vision let Daniel Pentland know that this was a dream and he began to fight against it as soon as he knew it was a dream, but it was already too late. Once the dream began to unreel there was no calling it back.

Amanda , Daniel's wife, heard him begin to dream and came wide awake. She slept lightly now, like a mother with small babies, though she had never slept so lightly when her sons were infants. Now she reached out and found that Daniel was sweating like a man in a fever. He groaned and thrashed and mumbled.

Amanda rubbed her hand down his chest and said, "It's OK. It's OK. It's only a dream, Danny."

The desert wind that never seemed to be still banged the Venetian blinds.

Daniel sat up suddenly, not awake and still struggling with the dream. Amanda threw her arms around him, pinning his arms to his side, and held him until he stopped struggling.

"Danny, are you awake now?" She asked after a moment.

"Yeah," he answered, his voice tightly controlled. "Did I hurt you?"

"No," she answered. The trembling that always followed the dreams was upon him now and she knew it was safe to ease her embrace.

Daniel drew a deep breath and let it out, glad he had not punched Amanda in his nightmare fight with Dr. Pest. Other times Amanda had not been so lucky.

The wind banged the Venetian blinds again and Amanda started to get up to pull them up but Daniel said, "No. Go back to sleep. I'll get them. I'm going out back."

It was 3:00 AM but Amanda did not try to get him to stay in bed. She knew he was afraid the dream would return if he tried to go back to sleep too soon.

Daniel rolled out of the bed. He was naked and took a moment to pull on some gym shorts that lay on the floor beside the bed, then he went to the window. He pulled the blinds up and let the moonlight spill in. It glowed from his sweat sheened body and Amanda thought how much she loved to feel that body beside her—in her. Their lovemaking had been joyful and passionate and fulfilling. They had only needed one another for so long— until Kit.

Amanda lay down again and pulled the sheet up to her chin. The dreams did not come as often now and some days Daniel seemed almost his old self, but then Dr. Pest would come in the night and Daniel would awake fighting. Sometimes that would end his sleep for days on end. She hoped this would not be one of those times because when he did not sleep she did not sleep, and that made her days in the Logistics office very long. It was times like these that she hated Daniel and when she let her hate get loose for a moment she felt guilty, knowing Daniel couldn't help what came into his dreams; knowing that she was at least partly to blame for what had happened. But then in the next second her anger would bubble up again and she would wonder why she stayed with this man who so clearly wanted Kit, whom he could never have. That thought was always followed with, *but if I leave him he would be dead within days.* She tried to convince herself that this wasn't true, that Daniel was better, less depressed, and less suicidal, but her heart knew it wasn't true. Even in the times he seemed better she could see through the brittle façade of wellness to the pain beneath. When the cycle of her thoughts reached this point, as it always did, she cried with frustration and anger and love for Daniel in spite of his sins.

Daniel went out to the patio and sat on the chaise lounge.

The wind dried the sweat of the dream and he shivered more. The yipping howl of the coyotes that prowled the open spaces of Edwards AFB wavered through the night and the lonely sound resonated in his chest. The moon made the night almost as bright as day and when he glanced up at the sky he almost wished he could howl at the moon like the coyotes, but then he might have missed Kit's voice on the wind. She had begun calling to him some weeks ago and he wondered if her voice on the wind was why the dreams had started coming more frequently. Daniel strained to hear it now but there were only the coyotes and the absence of her voice left him hollow.

Kit's real name was Gwendolyn Christopher Marlowe and Daniel had loved her from the first moment he saw her, sitting primly in St. George's church in Venice. Her shoulder length strawberry blond hair made a nimbus around her face. She glowed as though there was some incandescent filament in her. Clouds of Bach poured from the organ hidden in its loft at the back of the church. Amanda and Daniel, walking hand in hand, pushed open the bronze bound door and stepped through the curtain inside the foyer that was supposed to keep drafts out. It was not doing the job nor was the cranky steam heating system. The sanctuary was meat locker cold and would stay that way until the next summer.

Kit was sitting alone in the sanctuary. She was in the right row of pews toward the back and her head, bent over something she was reading, moved a little to the beat of the music. Wisps of vapor rose from her breath.

"Good Morning," Amanda said.

Kit, lost in the music, started at the sound of Amanda's voice and turned sapphire blue eyes behind granny style reading glasses to the Pentlands. Her face was creamy pale and kissed with a dusting of freckles. Daniel's heart melted at the sight of her.

"Oh, I'm sorry," Amanda said. "I didn't mean to frighten

you."

"No, No. Silly of me to jump. I should have been paying more attention," she said. Her accent was pure New Castle Jordie.

"Easy to get lost in the music," Amanda said. "You're new, aren't you?" Amanda and Daniel had been coming to St. George's from the American Air Force Base at Aviano two or three times a month for the last year. The last vestige of British power, St. George's Anglican had remained even when the active British Consulate had been made merely honorary. The fact that it was in Venice gave it a romantic cachet that made the effort it took to get up early and ride the train from Aviano to come to services, worth it. Amanda had already become proprietary of the Church.

"I got here Wednesday," Kit said. "I'm from England on a foreign study semester." Her blue eyes swept over the two of them, but rested a moment when they met Daniel's gaze.

"I'm Amanda Pentland," Amanda said and stuck out her hand. "This is my husband, Daniel."

"Gwendolyn Marlowe, but everyone calls me Kit," she said, shaking Amanda's hand then extending it to Daniel.

Daniel was speechless at first, only able to stare at this beautiful woman and try not to jibber or drool. He took her hand when it was offered. It was cold. With a surge of primal desire Daniel wanted to press that cold hand to his lips, but he restrained himself. His native smart assedness came to his rescue.

"Kit Marlowe, like the guy that wrote Shakespeare's plays?" Daniel asked smiling.

Kit grinned and lifted an eyebrow in answer. "Blasphemy!" she said. "Everyone knows Bacon wrote Shakespeare's Plays!"

Amanda laughed. "Please pardon my husband Kit, he can't help it. He's literary."

"Oh?" Kit said, "Are you writing something that may be

Shakespeare someday Mr. Pentland?"

Daniel shrugged. "More likely landfill any day now. Please call me Danny."

"That's not so!" Amanda said, a little more vehemently than the banter called for.

What a strange thing, Kit thought when Pentland called himself Danny. There was such a feeling of acquaintance that it caused a shiver quite apart from the cold to run up her spine. It was as though she were greeting an old friend. *No, not a friend, a lover*. A twist of apprehension went through her but, curiously, ended as a small shiver of desire. She covered it by jamming her hands into the pockets of her coat.

Daniel noticed. "Cold hands, warm heart," he said.

"Cold hands, cold feet is more like it," Kit answered, dancing a little against the chill. "It's colder and damper here than in England."

The sacristy door at the back of the church opened and the Reverend Canon Doyle, (who had heard *all* the Sherlock Holmes jokes when he was created Canon) stepped out. "I thought I heard voices," he said, his accent distinctly American. He was a tall, slender old man with thinning white hair and faded blue eyes. He was dressed in his usual black suit and dog collar with a heavy black topcoat over it.

"Good Morning Father," Daniel and Amanda said together.

"Good Morning, good morning," he answered. Tiny puffs of steam came from his mouth like cartoon balloons. His tenor voice always seemed to be on the verge of breaking into one of the operatic arias he loved. "I turned the radiators on about six this morning, but I'm afraid that is still not early enough. I suppose I shall have to begin turning them on Saturday night.

"How was the train?" He asked Amanda and Daniel.

"Not so bad. Wasn't crowded," Daniel said.

"Just wait. Carnival starts next week. Then everything will

be crowded. I am going to just stay home and lock the doors until the tourists go home," he said laughing.

"If we could just find some way to have them mail their money to La Serenissima and stay home themselves..." Daniel quoted the well known sentiment of most Venetians and they all laughed.

"So true," Doyle agreed. "I see you have met Kit."

"Yes," Amanda said smiling.

Daniel said nothing. Mention of Kit's name seemed to steal his mental control. He was sure he would babble like an idiot if he opened his mouth.

"So, how is the work going Daniel?" Doyle asked.

Pentland pulled his thoughts away from Kit and managed to answer with only a slight lag. "Not bad I guess. The words are going onto the paper. Now as to whether anyone will buy them—who knows? But I am managing to get the words onto the paper."

"I understand that is the hardest part," Doyle said. He always managed to make Daniel feel as though he really cared. Maybe it was just his job as a priest or something. Daniel never pushed to find out if the old man really did care or was just an accomplished faker.

"How is Elizabeth?" Amanda asked, referring to Doyle's wife, who was crippled with arthritis.

"Not so bad. She may be here this morning. The winter is so hard."

"Being this close to the water must make it worse," Daniel said.

"I have tried to talk her into letting me take her to Arizona or California where it is dry, but she won't listen. We love Venice so much."

Conversation stopped for a moment as the four of them thought of Elizabeth.

Doyle looked at his watch. "Well, where has the morning gone? I must go get my dress on. Can't keep the British Consul waiting. Assuming they get here this morning that is."

He turned and went back into the sacristy, and the door had no more than closed behind him when the Honorary British Consul and his wife came through the curtained door. "Good morning dear children," the Consul said, his voice full of cheer. "What of our American Allies?" He went on as though this were 1944 not 1994. He was short and stooped with thinning gray hair and faded blue eyes. His droopy cheeks were pink with cold and his nose, veined with years of formal toasts, was red. He wore a not quite threadbare camel hair topcoat over a well-tailored (and not too shiny) brown wool suit.

"Good Morning Sir Reg, Lady Ann," Daniel and Amanda said. "Have you met Kit?" Amanda continued.

"Why yes of course," Lady Ann said. "How are you this morning dear?" She was taller than her husband and seemed less worn. Her hair was iron gray and had been folded into a schoolteacher's French roll at the back of her head. The style made her look hawkish because her nose had become more beak-like over the years. Her eyes were black and sharp and her years had done nothing to dull that sharpness. She wore a long black shearling coat over a dark blue Channel suit that had been stylish twenty years before.

The small talk and soft Bach continued as a few more worshipers trickled in, said their good mornings, and went to their accustomed places in the church. So far as Daniel knew there were no bought pews in the church, or at least there were no nameplates on the pews, but everyone seemed to know their places as everyone sat in the same pews each Sunday. Usually that didn't bother Daniel. He came for the church service and one seat was as good as another, but this assigned seat business was not good today because the seat Kit had chosen was farther back and on the other side of the central aisle from where Daniel and Amanda usually sat. In other words Daniel couldn't look at Kit without turning around, and more than anything in the world Daniel wanted to look at Kit.

Amanda put her hand on Daniel's arm, the kind of intimate wifely gesture that married people make without thinking, and felt the tension in him.

"What's wrong?" she asked in a whisper.

"Nothing."

Amanda recognized it as a lie. Almost thirty years and two children with him had given her an infallible antenna on him, or at least she thought it had.

"She is pretty isn't she?" Amanda said.

Daniel turned and looked at Amanda, purposely giving a comic gape to the glance.

Amanda smiled. One of the most endearing things about Daniel so far as she was concerned was his ability to make her laugh. "Don't look at me like that. I could see it in your eyes the second we came in."

"Well fine," he said in mock disgust, "but you could leave me some illusion of privacy, don't cha know?"

"Not good practice. It might make you think you could get away with something, and that would just get you in trouble," she said lightly.

"Yeah, right."

Amanda patted her husband's hand. "It's OK. You can look all you want. Just don't touch."

Daniel smiled at that, but it was false. There was an aching desire beneath it. He wanted to stand up, walk over to the lovely English girl, and take her hand and leave.

His body responded to his thoughts and he turned to look back at Kit. His heart leapt to find that she was looking at him as well. Their eyes met and locked and Kit smiled. It was so dazzling the cold church seemed to warm because of it. There was communication between them. Daniel could feel it, but he wasn't sure what was passing between them.

The sanctuary bell rang twice and Daniel reluctantly tore his eyes away from Kit. The congregation stood as Father

Doyle came from the Sacristy and down the aisle to the Altar to begin Matins.

The service played down through the hymns and through the readings and through the ritual invocations of Body and Blood and none of it penetrated Daniel's mind. He could only think about, pray, that Kit would come with the portion of the congregation that went to the Pseudo-English Pub on the alley behind St. George's church after the service. He dared not hope that she might go with those who left the pub for a nearby restaurant for lunch.

When the last hymn was sung, and the last Amen said Daniel, in a trance, stepped out of his pew and across to Kit's place. He was going to try to be all sophisticated and devil may care, but Kit's smiling eyes wiped out that possibility. He did manage to ask if she was going to go for coffee.

"That would be super," she said. "Perhaps a little something to warm my feet too."

"Brandy. Brandy will do that," Daniel said.

"Or a hot bath..." Amanda said. The sound of her voice jolted Daniel as though she had whacked him on the back of the head. He had truly forgotten that his wife was there with him, but the sudden thump of reality cleared the clouds from his head.

"A hot bath would be lovely," Kit said. "I'm afraid I shall have to forego hot soaks for a time though. My flat—more like a hostel really—has only a shower bath."

Mental images of Kit beneath a shower nozzle flickered through Daniel's mind and were gone.

A little knot of people stood beside the door talking with Father Doyle. When Amanda, Kit, and Daniel reached him he said, "Kit, are you going to come to the church hall for coffee?"

She looked confused. "I thought we were going to a pub 'round the corner?"

11

Doyle smiled merrily. "Yes, that's the church hall."

Kit laughed. "I believe these Italians have the right idea," she said.

"About many things," Doyle agreed, grinning. "So, Amanda and Daniel, if you will please take Kit around to the pub, I will join you shortly."

Amanda looked around the empty sanctuary. "Oh, I just noticed, Elizabeth didn't make it."

"No, it doesn't look as though," Father Doyle said. "I'll pop 'round to the house to see that all is well and perhaps bring her along with me if she feels up to it."

"I hope she does," Amanda said.

"Me too," Daniel chimed in just a half beat late. Kit noticed that he was looking at her rather than at Doyle or Amanda, and the look made her feel good.

Amanda took Daniel's left arm, then Daniel offered his right arm to Kit with a smile. She hesitated a moment then returned the smile and took his arm.

***

Daniel did not go back to bed after the nightmare. He couldn't. He knew the dream would return so he sat on the patio and tried to shake it off—tried to shake off the memory of Kit, but sitting on the desert patio two years later, he still remembered as though it had been yesterday. It was as though the entire world had disappeared save the few cubic feet of space occupied by Kit Marlowe and himself. Nothing from outside could penetrate that. For that little while there was no Amanda, there was no Air Force, there were no grown sons, there was no novel, which was not going as well as he had told Father Doyle, there was nothing save Kit. They sat jammed together side by side at the small tables of the pub, their thighs touching from hip to knee. Both felt the magnetic pull between them. Even when the crowd thinned they did not move apart. Daniel thought that he had managed to make witty conversation during the rest of that afternoon, but truth be told, he did not remember anything but Kit's lovely face.

Then it was over. Daniel found himself sitting beside his wife on the train bound for Aviano and there was an aching loneliness in his soul. It sat right beside a jeering guilt.

II

Kit got lost walking back to her flat after the Sunday luncheon, which was odd. She seldom got lost, or even misplaced. She had studied the tourist map of Venice and had it firmly in her mind when she had left the flat. The knowledge had taken her unerringly to St. George's, but somehow it failed when she left the Ristorante after lunch, and she knew why. Daniel Pentland. For some reason the tall older man would not leave her mind.

No, not for 'some reason' she thought, for one reason. He had been totally and obviously smitten with her, and that was flattering beyond thought. Men didn't usually fall in love, or even in lust, with her at first sight. She thought herself too fat and plain with too many freckles for that, but Daniel didn't seem to think so.

But even if a man had ever managed to get past her looks, she thought, they found that she was dull and slow, but Daniel didn't seem to think so. He had listened when she talked, and when he asked about her studies he seemed genuinely interested in what she said. Daniel laughed when she made a joke, and told her that 'Kits' were a penny candy he had been fond of when he was a child. After that he had called her Sweet or Sweet Kit...

My little speckled cow was what David, her fiancé, called her sometimes if he was in a playful mood. Stupid fat cow was what he had called her when she made it clear she was not going to stay in England and give up her architectural studies just to help him buy the house they were living in at the time.

That took Kit's thoughts down a path worn smooth with travel over the last couple of weeks. She did not want thoughts of David to push into what had until then been a perfect day, but there seemed to be no help for it. He stood there in her mind now just as he had stood the day she had told him she was coming to Italy.

"Venice! Good God," he had said. "It's an open sewer! And you don't even speak I tai!"

"I've been studying the tapes since the first day I applied," Kit shot back.

That had stopped him for a moment, but only a moment.

"Oh do give up this nonsense Kit!" He had said. "You know you'll never finish it, and if you do you'll never find a job!"

"I already have a job," she said, "And they promise I can have it back when I return."

"Architectural Intern," he snorted. "You practically have to pay them to let you go there."

"They like my work!"

"They like your fat arse and your silly face. They laugh at your thinking you're going to be an architect. Stay here with me, get a real job and we'll buy this house and have a start."

That had hurt. It always did and David knew it. He had been using that sort of derision against her since they were children. However, in the midst of that fight she had rebelled and told him to stuff his house and everything else. "I have a chance to add the prestige of this Italian study to my portfolio and you are not going to scream me out of it!" She said.

That was when he had called her a Stupid Fat Cow. He had even raised his hand as if to hit her, but thought better of it and ended with the insult and walking away.

Now as she wandered through the beauty of Venice looking at the Euro-Moorish architectural fusion—and looking for some familiar landmark, she could feel strong and confident, but David had almost taken the heart out of her that day. He had been so angry and cutting it made her cry, but now, away from him and on her own, she felt she could do anything.

But, if he had said, "Marry me tomorrow Kit," I might have stayed she thought. If he had just done something to show me he wanted me for more than a second income, I might have stayed.

She shook her head at the thoughts and tried again to push them away. She had been all joy when she parted from Daniel at the restaurant, but that joy was fading fast.

Not for the first time she wondered why she still considered David her fiancée. She didn't love him, exactly; and he didn't love her. More he was normalcy in her life that had been there for all time. Since play school it had been Kit and David as a unit, until as an adult, he had hit her. Her father had beaten him bloody and the Kit and David unit was broken up. Kit went to stay with her aunt in Australia after that. She stayed and worked for six months in Sidney then took a job with a relief agency in Kenya for a year before returning to New Castle.

David had met her at Gatwick Airport with flowers, apologies, and promises never to lay hands on her again and she had taken him back. *Like an utter fool,* she thought. Their engagement had dated from that time, though it was not formal, and her parents, especially her father, told her that David was 'a bad 'un, and not to be trusted.'

Kit turned a corner and suddenly she was back in territory she recognized. She sighed with relief and then her stomach gave a glad jump and all thoughts of David went out of her head. Several steps ahead of her there was a tall man with a dark haired woman walking beside him and the thought that it might be Daniel and Amanda Pentland lifted her heart until she realized it wasn't them. Wasn't him. Wasn't Daniel Pentland.

Odd, she thought. Why would I be so happy to see Daniel, (she just could not think of him as Danny) an almost perfect stranger? But memory of those green gold eyes looking so deeply into hers from across the lunch table answered that question. He had been so attentive and so kind and so funny and so sharp...

Silly cow, she chided herself. He has a beautiful wife. He was just being kind to a stranger. *Why would he be interested in you?* But he had been, or seemed to be, and it made her feel bubbly inside. *David never makes me feel that way,* she thought, and her mind started back down the same paths it had just trod; but this time she stopped in the middle of the street and commanded herself, "I will not think about David now! I don't want to think of him. I want to think about Daniel," and this time she shoved David away so firmly that he actually left her alone.

***

The train ride back to Aviano from Venice was silent and tense for Amanda. Daniel was in one of his monosyllabic moods, closed and quiet. He never actually said, "Don't bother me," but it radiated from him like heat.

Amanda tried to push through that radiation, to call him to her again by sitting close and putting her hand on his thigh. The sexual implications of that sometimes caused Daniel's inward moods to evaporate.

"Remember the train from Milan?" she whispered. Daniel glanced at her but there was no remembrance in his eyes. They had ridden to the American Consul in Milan to renew a passport that was about to expire. It had not been a particularly romantic day dealing with the Federal bureaucracy and on the way home that evening Daniel had been closed into himself. Amanda had moved beside him, laid her hand on his thigh and her head on his shoulder as she was now. They had the compartment to themselves so she had moved her hand a bit higher up his leg and that had accomplished her purpose.

"Right here on the train?" Daniel had asked, smiling.

"I always wanted to play on a train with a handsome stranger."

"Oh well, I'll see if I can dig one up," he said and made as if to get up.

Amanda kissed him and brought one of his hands up to her breast. That stopped the teasing. Daniel returned the kiss hungrily. "I have needed that all day," he said.

They had pulled the shades on the windows facing the aisle, locked the door and made love in the dark compartment while the few lights of the Italian countryside flicked by. The kisses had been sweet. The coupling had made them one for a little while, shutting out everything else. It had been exciting and wonderful, but it did not work this time.

After a while, she gave up and moved back across the compartment. She took off her shoes and put her feet up on the seat beside her husband.

Amanda knew what was running through Daniel's mind and it worried her. The English girl was beautiful, sweet and witty; Daniel had been at his absolute, charming best in her presence. He had flitted and flirted around her with grace and the sweet sounds of laughter. Kit had flown with him in swoops and swirls.

Now Daniel's eyes were distant and unfocused, his arms crossed and his head tilted down. He was not a particularly handsome man, but he was attractive in other ways. He could be witty and charming at times (like this afternoon with the English girl, she thought again, and shoved that thought away) and when he turned his adoration on Amanda, it could melt her into a puddle. That used to happen often. He would sweep his eyes over her in that special way and her mouth would water with anticipation of his kisses. Even after years of marriage, her knees would still go weak, and the tingle of desire would run through her breasts and down; but that look had not come into his eyes much of late. Now sometimes the look of him was more of dread than desire.

Amanda knew she was not young and nubile any more. She knew she was still attractive though, with long legs, bright brown eyes and slim hips. Young men still made flirting chat with her, and she often heard that she did not look old enough to have been married for so many years, and especially not old enough to have two grown sons, but when she looked at herself in the mirror she saw that she was indeed old enough. There were worry and smile lines in her face that grew deeper each day. There was a droop to her breasts, which used to be perky and high. Two children had suckled there and they were responsible for the drooping breasts and many of the facial lines. But even with all that, Daniel was usually attentive and passionate, seldom missing a chance to sneak a little caress or pinch or kiss, besides being kind and gentle and compassionate.

And faithful. Above all, he had been faithful.

Daniel and Amanda Pentland had been lovers pulling together as a team for a long time—more than half her life in fact. They had gloried in one another. They had loved passionately and deeply, and their love had overcome huge obstacles including her resentment filled and hateful family. Daniel and Amanda had fought to be together; and for the life of their first son when her family wanted the child aborted. More than once Amanda had been afraid Daniel and her father would come to blows, but if they had, she would have stood beside Daniel. When the world around them had been hostile, they had been comfort, soul mate, friend and lover to one another and it had always been so until the last two years. The years here in Italy. These years had started out very well indeed, almost like a second honeymoon. For the first time ever they were without children. They were in a new and romantic place and it had been exciting. The first two months, they could not keep their hands off each other. For the first time since early in their marriage, they made love twice or three times a day, and then, for no apparent reason it stopped. Well, almost no reason. Amanda thought Colonel Tom Preston might have had something to do with it.

Colonel Preston, her boss, wanted to be a General. He

was a former fighter pilot, which made him as arrogant and demanding as a three year old, and left him incompetent to do anything save fly an airplane. Amanda was at his beck and call twenty-four hours a day. He would have had her camping in the office if he could. More times than she cared to remember, Preston had called in the midst of love and she had gone.

At last, when they had been interrupted for the third time in one evening by phone calls and Amanda had left her husband unsatisfied in bed to run to the office Daniel had said, "Jesus Christ, Amanda! I hope you're having an affair with fucking Preston! I'd hate to think you're leaving me here like this to go shuffle some papers!"

"Danny, it's my job."

"To Hell with your job! I told you to let the machine pick up the phone the first time, but you wouldn't do it. You just had to answer it!"

"He's a Colonel!"

"He's an incompetent demanding asshole that can barely shake his pee pee by himself and somebody needs to tell him so."

"Master Sergeants don't tell Colonel's they are assholes!" She said, vexed by the truth of what Daniel was saying.

"Then I'll tell him!"

"No!"

His eyes burned into hers. "Come back to bed. The world isn't going to end if Preston doesn't get his report until tomorrow."

"Danny, please. I'll be back in an hour."

"Right," he said dryly.

When she got back two and a half hours later Daniel was asleep. He hardly spoke to her for days after.

A great gaping emptiness opened in her as she thought about this, and Daniel's silence, emphasized by the rhythmic sway and rattle of the train, was like an enemy that must be fought back or it would swallow her.

21

"I'm going TDY (Temporary Duty) next week," Amanda said and wondered why on earth she had brought that up now!

Daniel looked up. An expression of resigned indifference in his eyes. "Where to?"

"Spain. Morone."

"Wish I could go too," he said, and Amanda saw that he meant it. It made her feel better that he did mean it. They had loved Spain when they were stationed there and especially southern Spain around Seville. "It'll be a lot warmer and nicer there than it is here," he said.

"I wish you could too, but it wouldn't be any fun for you. I'm going to be deploying a bunch of people and most of the move is going to be on me too, so I'm going to stay busy the whole time."

"Yeah. Figures," he said. "Is this real world or exercise?"

"Exercise, but with the mess in Bosnia boiling we could be doing it for real anytime now."

Daniel took a deep breath and let it out slowly. "If we do send troops are you going to have to go?"

"Troops or not I'm going to have to go pretty soon anyway. Our sight surveys are old and if we have to move a bunch of people through a bunch of landing fields we have to know what we are getting into."

"How come you have to go? I thought when you moved from packing parachutes to Logistics you wouldn't have to spend as much time TDY."

"If it wasn't for this Bosnia thing I wouldn't, but these people just will go on killing each other and we can't have that," she said with a disgusted twist in her voice.

"Yeah, right. 'Ya knew the job was dangerous when you took it,'" he said, and then clucked like a chicken. It was a sarcastic quote from the Super Chicken Cartoons that had taken root in Aviano American Air Force Base since the Balkans had brought the base from a quiet population of a thousand up to a teeming and crowded ten thousand in a

22

matter of months.

"At least you don't have kids to take care of anymore."

"There is that."

"And you are in Italy. Maybe you could take a trip to Rome or something? Just jump on the train."

"Yeah, like I'd go to Rome without you."

"No, really. You could."

"You wouldn't mind if I went without you?"

Amanda thought, *Yes I'll mind, but it will keep you away from her,* but she said, "No I don't mind. You can go and scout out the country so that you can be a tour guide when we go back."

Daniel stared at her silently for a long time, clearly not convinced, but at last he said, "Maybe I'll do that."

The week sped by and Daniel seemed to get over his closed mood. He did not mention Kit or Venice at all, just went about his routine of exercise and housework and writing. Amanda did notice that the writing was not going particularly well. She could tell because when she came home in the evening about 1700 Daniel was not at his desk. If it was going well he would usually keep working until about 1800.

Amanda liked Daniel's work. Even that part of it she did not understand she liked. It made her feel like a patron of the arts. She only wished someone would recognize how good his work was and publish some of it, but that had not happened much. Daniel had collected a thousand rejection slips and only a handful of acceptances, and Amanda hurt for him every time he got rejected. He swore it didn't bother him anymore but that was a lie. A rejected manuscript would come back and it would eat at him for days. He would cook extravagant meals and exercise extra hard and the two of them would find someplace to go on the weekends, even if it was only on a bicycle ride through the Friulian countryside. He would be extra attentive of her then and when they made love it would be desperate and grasping as if the physical coupling helped him rid himself of

23

the pain of rejection.

When the wound healed, the regular routine would return. He would get up to see Amanda off to work, then run down to the Base gym for a workout. Then to the market and post office or whatever other house business needed doing on the Base and return home to prepare a large Italian lunch. Amanda would come home at 12:30, eat lunch and return to work while Daniel cleaned up the kitchen and went to work in the office about 2:00. It was a boring but comfortable rut. A rut that was about to be disrupted by this Spanish TDY.

Friday morning they rose early, threw Amanda's bags into the trunk of the car and drove to the airfield terminal in silence. This was not a new thing. TDY's had been a part of life since the beginning of Amanda's career.

"How long are you going to be gone?" Daniel asked as they pulled into the loading zone.

"Should be two weeks, but you know how this goes. I'll call you or have the office call you."

"OK," he answered and got out to help unload the bags.

The area was crawling with men and women dressed in camouflaged BDU's (Battle Dress Uniform). Everyone scurrying along with some job to do and all aimed at getting the mission off the ground. Daniel was one of the few people there in civilian clothes, and he was the only man not in BDU's.

Staff Sergeant Billy Vincent, one of the guys from Amanda's office, was waiting beside a pile of baggage and said "Good Morning Sgt. Pentland." He ignored Daniel, not from any malice, but because spouses, male or female, were secondary equipment at that point. Now the focus was to get the personnel checked in, loaded, and wheels up.

"Sgt. Vincent," Amanda acknowledged. "Are we progressing?"

"So far so good" that was another sarcastic joke. It was what the people at each floor of the Empire State Building heard from the jumper who thought he could survive the jump.

Daniel put the "A" Bag he was carrying on the pile and turned back toward the car.

"OK," Amanda said. "I'll be back in a minute." She turned, caught Daniel by the arm and led him a little away from the bustle around the baggage heap and put her arms around him.

"I love you Danny," she said.

"That's good," he answered, and bent to give her the expected good-bye peck, but Amanda turned it into something more than a peck.

After a little Daniel pulled back. "Hey hey, that is no way to be. Leave your husband in this kind of condition," he brushed his loins against her so that she could feel his tumescence.

She grinned wickedly and thrust her hips forward in answer to his pressure. "I want you to have something to look forward to when I get back," she said.

The grin and the thrust made the small flame of desire grow a little hotter in Daniel. He could not help but grin in return. "You are an evil vixen. You grabbed me by the balls the first day I set eyes on you and you haven't let go since."

"And you better remember that too."

Daniel's grin faded to seriousness, and he pulled his wife to him in a tight embrace. "I love you Amanda," he whispered, and she knew he meant it.

After a little he leaned back, glanced over at Sgt. Vincent and said, "You better get over there. Looks like Billy is about to pee his pants."

"Just another earth shaking crisis to be handled," Amanda said. "It'll wait another minute."

"Preston must not be around."

Amanda flinched at the dig, but let it go.

"Be careful, OK?" Daniel said.

"Spain is like going home, you know that."

"Yeah, but make sure you remember that it isn't home, especially with all this Bosnia mess going on, not to mention the damn Arabs. Just be a little careful, OK?"

"You worry too much."

"Probably, but be careful all the same."

"I will. And you keep that—"she rocked her hips side to side "ready for when I get back."

He broke away from her and said, "I'll be ready, blue balls and all."

Amanda laughed, touched his cheek and turned toward Sgt. Vincent. "OK Billy," she said. "What's up?"

Daniel didn't hang around to hear the answer.

III

Kit sneaked into Daniel's dreams the first night after Amanda went TDY and that worried him. His reaction to the English girl had been much stronger than any other pretty girl he had noticed in a long time. This one was so visceral! He felt there was such a connection between them! It was the same as the connection he had felt the first time he set eyes on Amanda. It was love, and he knew such a reaction was dangerous. It could only end one way and that would be in complete frustration for him so he tried to put her out of his mind, but when he did manage to shove Kit away Amanda came to take the English girl's place. That was nearly as frustrating as the impossibility of Kit.

When Amanda was TDY Daniel often went to the gym to punch out his frustrations with her, Preston, and the Air Force in general on the heavy bag. He started his workout with a run to the gym, then did some Nautilus and finally asked Chief Shabaz, the NCOIC (Non-commissioned Officer In Charge) of the fitness center and a friend, to steady the bag for him.

Fifteen minutes later the Chief said, "Time!"

Daniel, deep into the mindless concentration of pounding the bag, did not hear.

"Time already Dan! You're killing me!" The Chief shouted and it got through to Daniel. He stopped punching and went into a slow cool down dance. He was soaked with sweat and now that the concentration was gone his arms and shoulders vibrated with exhaustion.

"Amanda must be TDY again," the Chief said.

That caught Daniel by surprise. "What am I, wearing a sign or something?" Daniel said, still dancing and pulling off the work out gloves. He danced toward the towel he had thrown on the floor.

"Might as well be. When Amanda is here you run and do the Nautilus. When she's TDY you punch the bag like it was personal."

Daniel laughed as he bent to retrieve the towel. "It is personal Chief."

"I don't want to know who it is you were hitting just now," the other said grinning.

"No you probably don't. It might constitute insubordination."

"Might at that. You ever boxed for real?"

"Naw. I grew up in Pacoima. That's the raggedy end of the San Fernando Valley. Fisticuffs didn't do much good. You go to fight there, it was always mean. You know? One guy walks away and one guy doesn't. Kick 'em in the balls or the knees as quick as you can to get it over with."

Chief Shabaz turned serious. "Maybe you oughta try fisticuffs Dan. Sometimes it helps to hit a real person."

Daniel looked at Shabaz. "Is it that obvious, Chief?"

Shabaz shrugged noncommittally.

"Maybe I will some time Chief," he said.

Daniel trotted home but as soon as he had showered and sat down at the computer to try to work, Kit came back to his mind and drove away the words he had been going to write so he gave up and tried to read. That was useless too and the hours dragged until he could go to bed. Kit was in his dreams again and Daniel woke early the next morning with the decision already made; he was going to give fate a chance to throw them together in life as well as in dreams. *Give fate another chance to have a little laugh at my expense is more like it,* he thought. Rain had started sometime in the night and looking out the window he almost changed his mind, but the thought of spending the day in the silent house staring at the blank computer screen was enough to push him out the door. Driving to the train station a local driver darted out in front of him. Daniel stomped on the brake so hard he went sideways on the rain slick street. It shook him and thoughts that maybe it was some kind of a sign crossed his mind, but after a few moments of sitting beside the road shaking he put the Fiat in gear and went ahead.

Slate gray haze with silver drizzle was all Daniel could see out the train windows. It didn't matter. He had no need to see the sights between Aviano and Venice. He had seen them before—studied them until they were sharp pictures in his mind. He could call up sun-drenched vineyards struggling in the rocky Fruillian soil, or net-covered Kiwi arbors any time he wanted them. He thought it odd that there should be so many Kiwis in northern Italy. There should be New Zealand Marsupials around kiwi arbors, not black and white magpies or cuckoo birds that sounded like a bass version of his mother's cuckoo clock.

What the hell am I doing here, he thought for the hundredth time since leaving home. *I should be sitting faithfully in front of my computer tapping out the great American novel, instead of going to Venice. This is perfect weather for writing! Got the house to myself and everything...*

To himself—

That was part of the trouble. He was alone again, and that was a mixed blessing. When he was alone it gave him time to think and write and do pretty much what he wanted, now that the kids were grown and off on their own adventures with Uncle Sam. Before Italy "Alone" had been a relative term. He used to say it meant that he had all the burdens of loneliness and none of the benefits of being alone. For sixteen years it had meant that Amanda was off on a temporary duty assignment again, leaving him alone with two children then, after Jack joined the Navy, with only Mitch. Now Mitch was in the Marine Corps in Japan, which left Daniel truly alone in Italy. For the first time in their Air Force career Alone meant Alone, benefits and burdens alike.

As the train made a momentary stop at a little town called Mogliano, two stops from Venice's Santa Lucia station Daniel felt anger and frustration again. There didn't seem to be a reason for it but there it was, and now it was mixed with the anticipation of yet more frustration to come. *This whole thing is stupid!* He thought. *Do you really think you are going to just stumble across Kit out wandering in the rain?* But the thought wouldn't go away and as he looked through the rain streaked glass to the people on the Mogliano station platform he found himself seeking a glimpse of bright hair in the crowd.

Silly bugger, he thought, unconsciously adopting a British phrase. *What would Kit be doing over here anyway? And anyway what would you do if she were? Jump her bones right here on the train platform?*

It was a tempting idea—

His inner dialogue stopped being dialogue and became a mental videotape in which Kit smiled with come hither grace and a return of the desire he radiated.

Daniel shoved the thought away. Not that he didn't want to continue in some fantasy with Kit, but the mental video that had come up was a stock scene. Sort of a standard clip, which was cut into the whole show of his life. It could be used against any background. The foreground action was always the same—Daniel plus desired target exchange smiles. Daniel goes right into his witty urbane mode thereby sweeping the female target off her feet and magically into bed.

The trouble with the stock footage was that if it ever came to reality (and it had a few times) when it came down to the deed, Daniel couldn't do it. He loved Amanda and no matter how much he might want to stray, he didn't. Usually when the moment was passed beyond all redemption he cursed himself for a fool and flayed himself with regrets at not having yielded to the temptation.

That's what he was thinking about now. But he wondered if he could have held to his vows and added another missed opportunity to his bag of regrets if he had truly been as alone with Kit as he had felt that Sunday. It was a thought that didn't bear too close an examination, and trying to stay away from it didn't help his mood any.

What I really need is to see Kit, he thought.

Three hours later Daniel was strolling through the rain drenched alleys of Venice, with his hat pulled down tight and his collar turned up against the cold drizzle. He carried an umbrella furled in his hand. He had given up trying to use it because the narrow, crooked streets of Venice were always crowded, and even more so in February with Carnival beginning, and the narrowness of the streets made it comically frustrating to try to keep an umbrella open. People meeting would stare into one another's eyes and see the same question, '*Do I lift my umbrella up to pass or lower it so the other one can go above mine?*' From the right vantage point umbrellas going up and down as strangers passed looked like some huge slapstick engine with multicolored pistons going up and down.

Strolling through Venice's foggy drizzle was hardly comfortable, but there was enough romantic nonsense in Daniel's soul to make it endurable. He glanced up from under the brim of his hat and noticed again how surreal it seemed for figures to loom up out of the foggy rain. It was soon after the beginning of Carnival and a little early for people to be in costume, but there were many who were and meeting black and white checkered Harlequins, or Banana nosed Dr. Pests added to the altered reality.

Daniel climbed to the middle of the Accademia Bridge and looked up and down the Grand Canal. The weather had not changed the usual traffic of the canals. Freight haulers, construction barges, delivery boats, all moved up and down in more or less orderly patterns while vaporettos—Venice's water buses, called Vaporettos (steamers) because they used to be steam powered—wallowed from pier stop to pier stop.

31

The Vaporettos were to be avoided at all costs so far as Daniel was concerned. They were always crowded and slow. He had found that with a decent city map and a good pair of shoes he could go anywhere in the city in less time than he would have wasted waiting on the next Vaporetto. He had recently picked up a novel set in Venice where the author had described the Vaporettos as 'darting here and there along the Grand Canal'. It had ruined the book. Vaporettos did not 'dart' They wallowed, they ploughed, they lumbered, they sloshed, but they did not under any circumstance 'dart'.

The Accademia Bridge was one of the three bridges that crossed the Grand Canal. It crossed near the Accademia Museum hence the name, but it debauched into a section of Venice called the Dorso Duro. It was not a part of Venice that drew many tourists once one got away from the Accademia, and that was what drew Pentland to it, or at least that was the acknowledged reason. Daniel knew the area restaurants and bars because St. George's was located in Dorso Duro. He had some vague idea of stopping into St. George's to see Canon Doyle. The unacknowledged reason was that St. George's was the place where he had first seen Kit.

***

Such a feeling of loneliness crushed in on Kit Marlowe that she was on the verge of tears from the moment she woke that morning. It was barely light and rain beat on the window like ocean waves. She lay curled in the narrow bed of her tiny room and felt sorry for herself. A part of her mind jeered at her for being home sick. *It isn't as though you have never been away from home you silly cow,* it said. But she was as home sick now as her first time away at Girl Guide summer camp.

I'll just call Mum, she thought, and the thought got her out of bed. She dressed and went down stairs to the telephone; dialed the string of numbers, and listened to the burr of the rings at the other end. Five rings. Six. Ten. No answer.

Where is everyone? She thought. Then the thought turned

into worry. *Where could they be at this hour?* She looked at her watch. It was 7:00 AM in Venice, which made it 6:00 AM in New Castle. They should be up and preparing to leave the house for the day.

Without thinking Kit dialed what had been her own telephone number. David answered after the first ring. His voice sent a shiver through her and she almost hung up without saying anything, but thought better of it and said "Hello David."

"Kit! How are you darling?" He sounded so happy to hear from her!

"I'm fine, David... I just telephoned to ask if you knew where my Mum and Da are?"

"Work I should imagine. I was just on my way to work myself. Where are you? At your parents?"

"I'm in Venice..."

"Oh Gawd, I thought perhaps you had given up that nonsense and come home like a sensible girl."

The derision in David's voice changed some of Kit's loneliness to anger. "I told you before I left that I was going to finish my schooling so just leave that alone and tell me where Mum is if you know."

There was a long silence, and at last Kit asked "Are you still there?"

"I've had enough of this shit," David said.

"Do you know where they are, or not?" Kit answered, keeping a tight rein on her anger.

"I don't know where they are, I don't care where they are, nor do I care anymore where you are. You can stay in that filthy Italian sewer and rot for all I care. Allison Redding is here to take care of me. She knows how to be a woman, not some damned crusader. She cooks and cleans and when we go to bed she fucks like she cares for me, doesn't just lie there like a dead cow. I'm finished with you, you stupid bitch. Finished!" Then he slammed the phone down.

Allison Redding? Kit thought, feeling totally betrayed. She had thought of Allison as a friend. *How could she? How could he? How long have he and Allison been... Surely a long while. Allison wouldn't simply... How could David just break it off like... just break off like that?*

Kit's mind stopped spinning with that question and a spark of relief flickered up in her. David was finished therefore she was free...

...And alone.

The crushing loneliness that had begun the morning returned and stole away the glimmer of relief she had felt the moment before. One of the constants in her life had just stopped being constant. One of the people she used to count on had betrayed her. She was free, but she was alone in a foreign place, and there was such despair in the thought that she felt it as a pain in her stomach. In that instant she needed to see a familiar face more than ever before in her life. Even Marcy or Cynthia her flat mates, relative strangers, would have brought her back to sanity, but both of them were already gone. She tried dialing her mother's telephone number again but still got no answer.

Oh God, where are they? she thought. *What am I going to do?*

***

Daniel descended the bridge into Piazza Accademia. The vendors and tourists and the rain made the small square seem jammed—oppressive and threatening somehow. Daniel could hardly breathe. Though his hands and feet were chilled and wet with the rain he suddenly broke out in a fear sweat that soaked his underclothes. He elbowed his way blindly through the mob, making several heads turn. He did not know where he was going; only that he had to get out of the mob. If he could have wished himself out of the Piazza Accademia and back to his office in Marsure at that moment he would have done it, instead he pushed into the refuge of an alley, narrow even by Venetian standards. But it was out of the crowd so he walked down it.

Twenty steps down the alley emptied into a tiny campo not more than a dozen steps wide. Across the campo was a sign that read BAR REDEMPTOR. The redeemer's bar.

Daniel grinned at the name and the sense of oppression evaporated. The rain even eased up. "If that isn't a sign from the gods I will never see one," he said aloud. "And I could sure use the salvation of a coffee and a cognac." He walked over and looked in the window. There were a few tables covered with paper table cloths on the left and the bar, a wonderful marble affair with an inlaid top that looked too classy for such a hole in the wall, on the right. One corner of Daniel's mouth lifted. *A clean well-lighted place,* he thought and stepped in. The bitter-rich aroma of coffee was so strong he could taste it.

The bartender was a small fellow with steel gray hair and steel rimmed glasses. He wore a white shirt and a long white apron. He smiled and said "Buon Giorno."

"Buon Giorno," Daniel answered as he opened his coat and tilted back his hat. He stepped to the bar and leaned his elbows on the inlaid top. Behind the bar and to the left was a large modern stainless steel espresso machine, a grinder/dispenser that allowed the bartender to measure the perfect amount of ground coffee into the twist lock brewing baskets, and a tamper to pack the coffee tight before it was locked into the machine. Demitasse and cappuccino cups and their saucers were stacked beside the coffee machine. Directly behind the bartender three shelves held bottles filled with different colors of liquor. To the right were stacked many different styles of glasses.

"Un Cafe e' un Cognac," Daniel said.

"Cafe Corretto?" the barman asked, wanting to know if Daniel wished the Cognac in the coffee.

"Non. Cafe Qui—" Daniel made a parenthesis of his hands and set them on the bar, "e' Cognac qui." he said and moved his hands a little to the right.

"Ah," the man answered and continued in Italian, "Coffee for the hands and Cognac for the feet." He lifted an eyebrow questioningly to see if Daniel understood.

"Exacto," Daniel answered. His Italian was accented more with Spanish than English. He was not really fluent enough to read or speak educated Italian, but growing up in Los Angeles among Spanish speakers and having spent three years stationed near Madrid had given him a grasp of Latinate tongues so that he could fake his way through Italian pretty well. Besides, the hands and feet joke was old.

The bartender nodded and turned to the coffee maker. He measured the coffee into the twist lock basket, tamped it, locked it into position, hit the start button and dropped a white crockery demitasse cup beneath the spout. It was done all in one smooth economical, dance-like movement.

As the coffee began to drizzle out the spout sending up clouds of fragrant steam he turned with the same grace, plucked a small balloon shaped snifter from the stack and set it on the bar in front of Daniel. A cognac bottle seemed to appear in the man's hand and he poured the brown liquor into the snifter, stopping just above the red line, which ran around the glass midway of the widest point of the balloon.

That finished he turned back to the coffee machine just in time to thumb the stop button and leave the coffee strong and fragrant with just a touch of brew foam around the edge. He placed the cup on a saucer, dropped a tiny spoon beside the cup, sat the cup beside the cognac and pushed the large copper lidded sugar bowl with its long handled spoons toward Daniel. The whole ballet had taken perhaps a minute and it had been a delight to watch.

Daniel lifted the glass, cradling it in the palm of his hand with the stem between his fingers letting it warm a little before he brought it to his mouth and sipped. The sweet, woody aroma burned his nose as did the liquid sting his tongue. A warm glow began to radiate from his middle. He breathed out contentedly and saw that the barman was smiling. He smiled back and said, "I may need a whole bottle of Cognac for my feet today. It is hard to tell the Campos from the canals."

"It isn't so bad. In the spring the high tide came and flooded Piazza San Marco."

Daniel nodded. He and Amanda had come down to see the flooding. They had bumped and tiptoed across the flooded square on the narrow plank bridges the city resorted to several times a year.

"La Serenissima will sink beneath the Lagoon someday," Daniel said.

The barman nodded in sad agreement.

Daniel sipped at his cognac and looked out the windows onto the Campo. The rain was falling harder again. "What Campo is this?" He asked.

"Campo Redemptor.'

"Seems a pretty important name for such a small Campo."

The other shrugged. "The Redeemer was not such a great man to look upon, and yet see how much was accomplished by him?"

Daniel glanced back at the bartender to see him smiling gently. It warmed Daniel's heart as much as the cognac was warming his stomach.

"Your point is well taken," Daniel said glancing out the window again. The rain was beating so hard it was difficult to see. He felt sorry for the poor person who had just come into the Campo.

His heart lurched in disbelief and his mind denied the possibility.

It was Kit!

His mind denied it again. It was just some trick of the rain grayed light. Impossible… And yet it was her. She looked near drowned in a shapeless sack of a gray raincoat and a wad of tweed hat that looked like it would come apart any second.

Daniel shot from the bar and to the door without a heart

beats hesitation. The barman said, "Signor? The coffee—"

"Be right back," Daniel said and ignored the "But Signor… " that followed him.

She was just coming near the bar's door, head down, coat collar pulled tight, when he said, "Kit? Is that you?"

The girl stopped and looked out from beneath her dripping hat brim. Her face was like a Botticelli angel with the rain making it reflect. Her eyes were still beautiful sapphire blue, but they seemed swollen, as if she had been crying. She didn't seem to recognize him and that hurt. Perhaps all that connecting he had felt was just his fevered imagination.

Kit could not believe what she was seeing. The man who had been so much in her thoughts for more than a week was standing before her just when she needed him most. She threw her arms around him and crushed her face to his chest like a frightened little girl seeking protection.

The sudden embrace took Daniel so much by surprise that he almost tried to pull away, but he caught himself and put his arms around her. It was a miracle. All his dreams and wishes of days passed had suddenly come together here in this rainy Venice Campo.

"Kit, what's wrong? Are you alright?"

Hearing her name in this man's mouth released the words she was thinking. "I needed you so much," she said clinging tight and talking to his chest.

Daniel's knees felt rubbery. "Let's get out of the rain," he mumbled and turned with a protective arm around her. She was reluctant to let go her hold on him.

The barman had been watching everything and he ushered Kit and Daniel to a table. "Cognac Signor?" He asked.

"Yes. Two."

Daniel helped Kit out of her dripping coat and hat. He laid them on a chair. Her clothes and shoes were soaked too but there was not much that could be done about that at the moment. He felt as though he was dealing with an injured child. She was shivering as though she would never be warm again.

The cognac arrived and Daniel put one in Kit's hand then lifted hand and glass toward her mouth. Her lips were blue with cold. "Go ahead, drink it. It'll help warm you. Make you feel better."

She sipped the cognac and grimaced at the taste and the burn of it. Daniel, unthinking, reached up and pushed a strand of wet hair that had been plastered to Kit's forehead up out of her face. Her skin was cold and clammy.

"Now can you tell me what's wrong?"

Kit looked at him over the rim of her glass and she blushed, just realizing that, no matter how much this man had been in her dreams, he was still a relative stranger, and she had thrown herself into the arms. "Oh God," she said. "I'm so sorry Mister... Mister…"

"Mister. Mister?" Daniel asked confused. "A minute ago you were so glad to see me it broke my heart, and now you're calling me Mister?"

"I'm sorry—"

"Stop that," he answered with a grin. "I'm not sorry. I'm never sorry to be hugged by a beautiful girl. And my name is Daniel, not Mister."

Kit looked into her cognac and blushed. "I know," she said. "I just thought you wouldn't like a stranger calling you Daniel.

Her words went to his heart. She remembered him.

"Sweet Kit, you may call me anything you like," he said. "And you may hug me anytime you feel inclined."

Kit looked deep into Daniel's eyes. They were true hazel, deep green with golden flecks in them. She found real concern in them and something else she did not recognize, something dangerously attractive.

"I was so glad to see you," she began. Her voice broke and the tears began to trickle from her eyes.

Daniel took her hand. "No, it's all right. Don't cry." Unthinking, he brought the hand to his mouth and tenderly brushed his lips against her fingers. "It's OK. It's OK." He said. He felt so protective of her! At that moment he knew he would fight armies to save her, and he wanted to kill whoever it was that had hurt her so. He hadn't felt this way for a long time. He used to feel this way toward Amanda and his sons when they were children, but the feeling had gone so long ago that he could not remember when.

The feeling of strong hands and soft lips against her cold fingers sent warm electricity through Kit and it echoed against the memory of the attraction she had felt for this man on their first meeting. She had thought that attraction was purely physical and she had found it odd to feel so attracted to a man old enough to be her father. Now he was kissing her hands in the most natural way.

After a moment or two Daniel took Kit's hand away from his lips, but he did not let go of it. "Tell me what's wrong," he said.

"Oh no, I don't want to burden you with this. It is silly anyway." She said.

"It isn't silly if it hurts you as much as it seems to."

"Oh but it is! It was just silly homesickness. I do mean silly. It isn't as though this is my first time away from home for God's sake. I'm twenty-six years old and I've been round the world alone. I haven't lived at home, I mean in my parents' home, for years."

With the hyper-natural sense of one totally attuned to another Daniel knew she was not telling the whole truth. There was homesickness yes, but there was more. "Homesick isn't silly," he said. "It is terrible to feel suddenly alone and deserted."

"Yes! That is why I was so glad to see you! I felt so alone, so cut off from everything."

"Glad I could be there, but…" he hesitated not wanting to

spoil this moment, but wanting to help Kit; to stop her hurting. "There's more to this than simple loneliness isn't there?"

Kit again looked into his eyes and felt the warmth of his hand still holding hers and wanted to tell him everything about her. She looked down into the almost empty cognac glass. "I called my fiancée this morning," she began and felt a slight withdrawing of Daniel's grip, but that was all. She did not feel the clammy hand of reality that gripped his heart at hearing her say *fiancée*. But the heart squeeze was there and gone and it did not alter his desire to protect her.

"We had been living together before I got this chance to come here to study, but when I told him it upset him. He wanted me to stay in New Castle and quit my studies and find a job that paid more than an intern in an architecture firm."

"So that you could get married, right?" Daniel said.

"Not precisely," she answered with a dry twist in her voice. "More so that I could help him buy a house there in New Castle. I told him then that I wanted to finish my studies and did not want to get tied down to a house until that was done, but he didn't understand that." A flash of anger rose up in her. "Sometimes David can be such a selfish shit! He has always been that way, since we were children."

"There is nobody in the world who can hurt you like an old friend who turns out not to be as much of a friend as you thought."

Kit had not seen such a look of concern for her from anyone for a long long time, and especially not from David. The look made her shiver.

"Well, we didn't part on the happiest note, as you can imagine. He didn't even come to see me off." She stopped.

Daniel waited but when she didn't continue he said, "...And," to prod her along.

"I rang him up this morning. He said he was seeing someone else and I could stay in Italy for the rest of my life for all he cared." The anger was gone leaving only the hurt. Tears clouded her eyes again and began to roll down her face. Daniel once more lifted her hand to his lips then pulled her to him and engulfed her with his arms. "It's OK Kit. It's OK," and as he comforted and felt the tiny shudders of her body as she cried— as he held her and tried to make her hurt less his heart was rejoicing! He could hardly stop himself from singing out his joy that this David was such a fool! For the moment his joy pushed out all thought that he was not as free as Kit was. He only remembered from the deepest well of his being this feeling of being needed on the most elemental level, where his very presence was the tonic most needed by another being. He stroked her still wet hair and lifted a strand of it to his lips. He was almost overwhelmed by the need to kiss her mouth, but he was afraid it would frighten her. He would have cut off a hand rather than frighten or hurt her.

At last Kit stopped shuddering and brought her face away from Daniel's chest. She looked up into his eyes and the desire to kiss him was a coppery taste on her tongue, but she held herself back remembering that she had liked Amanda, his wife. She pulled herself away from his arms and regretted the loss of their warmth the instant after. She wanted to fall back into their shielding, but knew she shouldn't. "I must look a fright," she said, taking her hand away from his grip to push her hair back.

Daniel felt bereft and empty. He wanted to take her hand back into his own, to pull her back into his arms, but he didn't. "Not so bad," he answered, trying not to let his regret show.

"You wouldn't happen to have a tissue would you?"

Without thinking the joke sprang from Daniel's mouth— "Tissue? Why I hardly know you." And he was instantly sorry for it finished breaking the mood.

Kit laughed.

"I'm sorry," Daniel said, grinning sheepishly. "Sometimes these things just pop out of their own volition. And I don't have a tissue." He turned to the bartender, who had been keeping a discreet distance, and asked.

"Oh si, Signore." He came out from behind the bar and brought them a small package of tissue.

Kit wiped her eyes and nose, but felt that she needed more so she excused herself and stood.

Daniel, not usually a victim of courtly manners, stood too.

"Do you have a ladies room?" She asked in passable Italian.

He smiled and gestured down a little hall that ran deeper into the building toward the kitchen.

"Thank you, "she said and turned that way.

"Would you like another cognac?" Daniel asked.

Kit turned back and made a face. "No thank you. But I would like a Cappuccino."

"I'll see to it."

She smiled at him and went.

Daniel stepped to the bar. "Due' cappucini, e' un cognac piu" he said.

The bartender turned and began his coffee ballet again, but this time in the midst of the dance he asked, "Is the Signorina all right now?"

"Her heart is broken, but I think she will heal."

He nodded and turned to pick the cognac bottle from the shelf. He poured until the amber liquid was just above the red line around the glass. "Who would break the heart of such a beautiful woman?" He asked rhetorically, shaking his head.

"It is hard to understand, isn't it?"

"Such a lovely thing should be protected."

Daniel nodded his agreement.

The steamed milk was poured into the coffee when Kit reappeared, looking refreshed. Her eyes were sparkling again though they still showed signs of weeping.

She came to the bar. "Better now?" She asked.

Daniel smiled. "That is a loaded question," he said lightly. "That is a question a woman asks a man when she wants to make him squirm."

"How so?" she asked and put sugar in her coffee and stirred it.

"No matter how a man answers that question it could be taken wrong if the woman wants to be nasty. If I said, why yes you look so much better, you could come back with, oh did I look so much like a witch before? Even I would not be so foolish as to say, No you looked better before, even if it was true."

Kit smiled and took a sip of her coffee. The thick foam of the milk left a thin line on her upper lip, but the point of her tongue darted out and across and the foam was gone.

"Do you live over here on the Dorso Duro?" Daniel asked, trying to keep it light even as his hands itched to reach out and take hers.

"No, I live over near the university in a flat with two other girls." She felt the next question before it was asked and said, "I tried to telephone my mother in New Castle, but she wasn't home, and that really got the wind up for me so I came over here to talk with Father Doyle, but he wasn't at the church or at home either. That was what finally caused my hysterics I think. I had managed to, more or less, maintain my composure until no one answered at Father Doyle's house. Then I just started walking."

Kit frowned and looked from her coffee to Daniel's face again, "But you are the one who is far out of his socket. What are you doing here? You live in Pordenone don't you?"

"Aviano. Well, a little town called Marsure actually. Right up against the Alps. And as for what I am doing here, the conventional answer is that I came down to have a look at the beginning of Carnival, but—" he hesitated a second, considering, then decided to go on. "I think the real answer is that I was looking for you." The words were out of his mouth now and he could not call them back even if he wanted them back.

Kit felt an irrational tingle of gladness at that. "Certainly sounds very Greek. Fate and all. I'm not sure I believe in fate but, at the same time, you were here when I needed someone, no matter what the reason. I don't know what I would have done if you hadn't called my name."

Two years later, sitting in the growing light of the Mojave's dawn, Daniel wished above all things in the universe that he had not called her name on that rainy day in Venice.

IV

The rain let up as the afternoon passed, but Kit and Daniel didn't notice. BAR REDEMPTOR was warm and not crowded and Giorgio the bartender was there to bring them what they wanted. They ate lunch then sat sipping their wine and talking for hours. They were at ease in each other's presence. There was a sexual tension between them that was like perfume on the air, yet they were as comfortable with one another as though they were old friends.

Kit was luminous, like a painting of a Celtic Goddess. Her face shone so that Daniel was sure he could have seen her in the dark. He tried hard to steer his thoughts away from his train fantasies, but those phantoms mixed with reality and hovered about him. His body remembered Kit's body, warm in his arms; the taste of her skin; the smell her hair; her breasts pressing against his chest; and her delicious presence was right there in front of him, deep blue eyes shining, dawn-tinted lips smiling. It was an agony to sit so close to her that he could simply lift his hand to stroke her cheek yet not be able to do it.

All at once, Daniel's tortured thoughts focused on what Kit was saying.

"I've been engaged to David since I can remember," she said.

Envy and despise for this David rose into his stomach to sour the wine he had been sipping.

"I think it happened when we were children," she continued. "He was the boy next door and it just seemed natural that we should be married."

"Maybe that is the trouble," Daniel said, a little of his bile leaking into his tone. "The saying goes, 'familiarity breeds

47

contempt'."

Kit looked sharply at him for a moment. "Yes I suppose so," she said and glanced out the window. "Oh look. The sun," she said. Red-gold streaks of late afternoon light pierced the clouds and made tiny Campo Redemptor glow.

"I should be getting back to my flat," Kit said. "But I really don't want to. It will be lonely."

"You have roommates don't you?"

"Yes, but they are strangers."

"I'm a stranger," Daniel said, then wanted the words back.

Kit smiled. "Not anymore She pushed back her chair and reached over to pick her coat and hat off the other chair. She made a face when she touched them. They were still soggy.

"At least my clothes are dry," she said, and stood. She made as if to put the damp coat on, but thought better of it.

"You really mean to go?" Daniel asked with regret.

"Yes, I'm afraid I must." She turned and said "Giorgio, the bill please."

"Si Signorina," he answered and began writing figures on a pad.

In his mind, Daniel rummaged for some word that might keep her from leaving but found only an inanity to fill the silence. "It always amazes me when these bartenders do that," he said. "I doubt if he wrote anything down this whole afternoon, but he'll remember everything."

"Yes, unfortunately. This wonderful afternoon has crushed my budget for the week I'm afraid."

"No it has not," Daniel denied. "This is all going to be on me."

"Oh I can't let you do all that! Women's Liberation and all."

"No."

"But I must insist—"

"No!" And on the instant, Daniel saw a way of staying

48

with her a little longer. "But I'll tell you what. At the risk of offending your feminist aspirations— if you will let me walk you home we will call it all square."

Kit looked into those smiling hazel eyes and felt the danger there. The pressure of them sent shivers down her body that gathered in a puddle just beneath her heart and excited her. She was a little afraid, but the coppery taste of desire was once more in her mouth and she smiled.

"Well then, at the risk of losing my feminist credentials, and preserving my budget, I agree."

As if on cue, Giorgio brought the bill. Daniel paid it, thanked Giorgio profusely and they went out.

The last of the streaky sun was lost to clouds and evening. The air was damp and chilly and Kit shivered. With her coat being wet, she knew it would be pointless to put it on so she reconciled herself to being chilled to the bone before she could get inside again.

Daniel had put his raincoat back on inside the bar, but when he saw Kit shiver, he took it off and draped it around her shoulders.

Kit looked at him in surprise. Such gestures had never been a part of her life. "You'll be cold," she said.

Daniel smiled. "The proper gallant answer for that is, better that I should freeze than that Milady should feel a chill, but the fact is I'm dressed a lot more warmly than you and I didn't get soaked to the skin. I don't really need the coat."

Kit saw that he meant what he said, and the coat was still warm from him. "Well then, thank you." A bitter little laugh came to her. "I can't ever remember David doing anything like lend me a coat."

Daniel wanted to say something cutting about the hated David, but kept his mouth shut. He didn't want to give Kit any reason at all to come to David's defense.

***

Amanda looked up and down the interior of the C-130

Hercules— at the crate taller than she was chained to the slip rails in the center of the plane, and then at the rest of her team, each deep in their own thoughts. She was the only woman and she was in charge.

What the hell am I doing here? She thought. *I didn't sign on for combat!* But here she was about to make a combat landing and off-load at Sarajevo Airport.

Amanda did not have to be here. She had not been ordered or even asked to do this mission, but since she was a former parachute packer/ cargo handler and had combat off-load experience, though it was only practice, when the opportunity came she jumped at it. The C-130 had been diverted from the Spanish exercise to deliver medical supplies and a kidney dialysis machine. The supplies were for the IFOR (International Peace Keeping Force) troops that were occupying Sarajevo. The dialysis machine was so that Colonel Preston might someday become General Preston. The dialysis machine was going into a Sarajevo hospital so that some people who needed it would not have to be shipped to a less dangerous part of the world to receive treatment. It would look very good on Preston's next OPR(Officer Proficiency Report) that the team he commanded jumped into the breach when needed, just as it would look very good on Amanda's APR(Airman Proficiency Report) that she had volunteered to head up the off load team.

The Sarajevo Airport had been closed for weeks, but a C-130 didn't need tower assistance to land, only a flat strip and good intelligence. That intelligence said that since the Airport had been closed, the shelling of it had stopped, and the runway had been repaired. In truth the landing and the off load should be a piece of cake, but that did not stop Amanda's stomach boiling with fear. Not so long ago hostile strangers had been shooting at anything that moved on the runway and just because they seemed to have stopped there was no guarantee that they truly had. She understood now what some of the

Vietnam combat veterans meant by "a high pucker factor" mission. She felt as though she might soil herself if something went wrong.

The pucker factor went up a notch when the C-130 engines changed sound and the plane nosed over into a steep descent.

"Here we go Sgt. Pentland." the pilot's voice came on the command channel of the intercom. "You got your asshole tightened up?"

Amanda laughed despite her fear. She had been dealing with male chauvinism since she was a parachute packer and it hadn't gotten any better since she had become a Logistics weeny. "So tight you couldn't pull a needle out Captain," she answered.

Now the captain laughed and opened the general intercom channel. "About five minutes guys."

Amanda didn't even think to correct the pilot on his 'guys.' She was the team leader and one of the guys right now. She looked around at her team and gave a questioning 'thumbs up.' The other three answered with their own 'thumbs up' that meant they were ready to go.

The promised five minutes were gone in a few heartbeats and the pilot said, "Here we go–" just as the screech of the wheels touching down penetrated the scream of the engines.

The thrusters reversed and the plane shuddered and began to slow. The ramp door at the tail opened a crack and began to lower just as the screech of the wheels touching down grew louder than the scream of the engines.

The team unstrapped and stood ready to break loose the chains, which held the pallet in place. Only Amanda was still hooked into the intercom. All eyes were on her to give the signal.

Amanda was breathing as though she had just run a thousand meters and fear sweat slicked her face.

The ramp was almost down and the plane was almost

stopped when the pilot shouted "GO, GO, GO!"

Amanda echoed the command and circled her arm like a windmill so there could be no misunderstanding. She threw off her Mickey Mouse ears as the team broke the chains loose and shoved the pallet down the rails. It reached the door just as the ramp touched the runway. The plane was still moving at a mile or two per hour when the pallet bumped onto the runway.

So far so, so good Amanda thought looking around. There was supposed to be a forklift waiting but she did not see it at first, and then it was there.

"Vincent! You three back on the plane!" She shouted and pointed both arms at the tail ramp, which was continuing slowly down the runway.

The others acknowledged and headed for the plane at a run.

Amanda turned to the forklift and directed the driver's placement of his tines to slide perfectly beneath the pallet then jumped out of the way.

The tines slid in and Amanda gave a 'thumbs up' when the pallet was resting tight against the uprights. The pallet lifted and she pointed both arms back toward the way the forklift had come. Without waiting to see if the driver turned or not she began running toward the still slowly retreating plane ramp. The other three were just getting to the plane and one of them stumbled as he stepped onto the barely moving ramp.

Sergeant Vincent grabbed the man—*must have been Conley*, Amanda thought—by the collar of his flak jacket and hauled him upright again. The three continued into the plane.

The ramp lifted an inch from the runway and was about six inches up when Amanda reached it. Vincent and Jaworski stretched out their arms and when Amanda leapt up onto the ramp they grabbed her by the armholes of her flak jacket and pulled her in.

Conley had the com-set Mickey Mouse ears on and was shouting into the mike but Amanda could not hear what he was shouting. It must have been something like the pilot's earlier "GO, GO, GO," for the engine noise increased ten-fold and the ramp closed faster.

The team struggled against the movement of the plane, got themselves into their sling seats, and strapped down just as the C-130 began making its turn for takeoff.

The team looked around at one another and all four were grinning like idiots. The whole off load had gone like clockwork and taken about two minutes. Amanda felt like screaming for joy.

The sound of the first shell landing near the plane barely got through the scream of the engines but it was enough to let them know what was happening. The C-130 kept moving though. No damage. More shells fell and Amanda felt her bladder control slip, but she was too scared to worry about dignity.

The engines were at full rev and all thought they were going to make it when a final shell hit close with a bang so loud and a concussion so strong it shook the plane. Suddenly the noise of the engines was cut in half. One engine was down. Smoke rolled into the cargo compartment and the pilot began shouting, "We're hit! We're hit! Get out! Get out! Head for the tower! There's a bunker there!"

***

Kit and Daniel strolled through the narrow darkening streets not noticing the crowds, but much affected by them all the same. That knowledge was pushed out of their reality by their acute awareness of one another. The effect was that if they brushed against one another there was an invisible arc of electricity, which jumped between them, and the crowd forced them to brush and bump together a lot.

More and more costumes were abroad though it was only the second day of Carnival. There were many clowns and some modern TV and cinema characters, but the classics of the Commedia dell' arte were still present. Petrucchio,

53

Braggidocio, Columbina, Harlequin. Doctor Pest with his long nosed mask and ground dragging black cape, were well represented. The characters were loved because of their proclivity for bawdy romance and laughter.

Near the university Kit and Daniel turned down a narrow alley, which was Kit's street. At first the street was empty of revelers, but they had hardly taken ten steps when four commedia characters appeared ahead of them. Harlequin, in his checkered costume, Dr. Pest, with his cape and long nosed mask, Columbina with her wide skirts, and Braggadocio, the Lustful, cowardly captain. They were laughing and dancing and taking every inch of the street.

There was a convenient niche beneath a streetlight in the wall on the left only a half dozen steps from Kit's front door. Daniel stepped into it and pulled Kit in with him, intending to let the little parade pass, but they didn't pass. They stopped before the niche and began making gestures and talking gibberish toward the trapped couple. At last Columbina and Harlequin leaned toward each other and stuck out there lips in an exaggerated kiss, then drew back and laughed. They turned toward the two in the niche and made get together gestures with their hands.

Braggadocio, less romantic, wiggled his eyebrows and then humped his hips several times.

Kit and Daniel both shook their heads, but Columbina and Harlequin ignored the protest and continued their demonstration, as did Braggadocio.

Dr. Pest, who had just been watching, tapped his long stick on the cobblestones, then lifted it and poked at Kit and Daniel, checking to see if they were dead, as if they were plague victims found lying in the street.

Kit and Daniel's toll for being free from the niche and passing on their way was going to be a kiss and there was no help for it.

Daniel leaned down and brushed his lips against Kit's

forehead, then looked out.

Columbina was standing, arms akimbo tapping her foot impatiently. Harlequin was shaking his finger back and forth, clearly saying 'not enough' by it. Braggadocio stopped his humping but wriggled his fingers in anticipation and moved toward Kit as if to say; well if you are such a fool as to leave her unkissed, I am not!

Dr. Pest lifted his stick and knocked it against Braggadocio's leg, then made a forbidding finger waggle with the other hand.

With much comic fuming the captain backed off. But then Doctor Pest did a strange thing, out of character. He lifted his stick behind Daniel's back and pushed him toward Kit with it.

This time Kit lifted her face and Daniel brushed his lips over her lips. The touch was tiny, almost negligible, but it caused a watery melting of Daniel's heart. He wanted to take Kit in his arms and really kiss her, but he didn't. After the quick kiss he looked toward the players.

Columbina still had hands on hips, but she wasn't tapping her foot any longer. Harlequin had a twisted, thoughtful look on his painted face. Braggadocio was leering even more and inching toward them. Dr. Pest tapped on his stick with his fingers, as though considering. They were saying, well, that's better, but still not enough.

After a moment Columbina stepped up to Daniel. She took his hands in her own, turned him a little and insinuated herself into his arms. She turned her face up to him, put her arms around his neck and pulled his face down and planted a big sloppy wet comic kiss on his lips, smearing it around to cover his whole mouth with her lipstick. Braggadocio licked his chops and started for Kit, but Harlequin grabbed him by the collar. Columbina stepped back and nodded with a satisfied little jerk of her head.

Harlequin, with Braggadocio's collar still in his hand, was looking at Columbina with wide eyed shock. His mouth stood open and he began to berate her silently with a wagging finger. She shook her head haughtily and turned toward Kit and Daniel, again making get together gestures.

It was as though the gods had destined this to happen and had sent these creatures of comedy to force the issue. Daniel took a deep breath and looked down to find Kit's face already turned up to him, her eyes half closed, lips slightly parted. He put his arms around her, leaned down and kissed her.

The sensation of his lips against hers was galvanizing. It stole Kit's breath and lifted her arms to go around him though she had no conscious thought to do so. Her heart leapt and cried and melted all at the same time. The taste of his kiss cascaded through her and her soul cried, *This is how a man's kiss should taste. This is how his arms should feel around me.*

Daniel felt the kiss beneath his heart like a blow mixed of wonder, desire and dread. Even as the warmth of Kit's mouth consumed him, made him hunger for more kisses, he knew this was a cosmic deceit; a divine prank that would bring both he and Kit only pain, but to hold Kit in his arms even for a few moments more he would willingly play comic relief to the universe.

When the kiss ended they did not part, but stood in the niche beneath the light holding one another, entangled in the moment. Kit's head was against Daniel's chest and she could hear the beating of his heart. Daniel's face was down, breathing in the perfume of her hair, lips touching the top of her head in a protective kiss. They did not notice when the comedy troop moved away.

"I love you Kit," Daniel whispered, half hoping she could not hear what he could not help saying.

"No Daniel, No!" She said holding him tighter. "You can't. You can't! And I can't love you."

He tilted her face up to his again and saw that she was crying, and each tear was like a drop of acid on his soul. He bent and kissed her eyes. "Don't cry sweet Kit. Don't cry," he said, then kissed her mouth again. They could not part. They could only stand beneath the light in each other's arms and wish that the moment would go on forever. The rain began to fall once more. Daniel took his arms from around Kit for a moment and opened his umbrella over them. "We must get you out of this," he said looking around for a bar or restaurant. But there was nothing.

The concern for her in his voice made her feel warm and cared for. "I can't go back to my flat Daniel, not now. Not yet." Kit said. She had just found this man. She did not want to let him go so soon, and yet—

Daniel's heart leapt to hear that, but trembled in the next second. He wanted her with body, mind, and soul, but that wanting could destroy him. Amanda flickered through his mind and was gone.

"But there is nowhere else," he said. "Every hotel and guest room in Venice is full. It's Carnival."

Kit pressed herself against him more tightly. "Maybe that is best," she said.

Something in Daniel's mind said *Yes, it is best,* even as something in his soul cried out *NO NO NO!*

Rain was running from the umbrella like a waterfall. It echoed in the narrow street with a pounding loneliness that caught at Daniel's throat. "Come on," he said. "Let's get you home."

Kit's flat was only a few yards farther along on the right. There was a dooryard so small that Daniel's umbrella almost covered it like a roof. Kit tried the door handle and found it was unlocked. "My flat mates are home, at least one of them. I hoped..."

"The gods aren't going to be that kind," Daniel said. *Or that cruel,* he thought. "Go in the house Kit. I love you, and I want you, but," he shook his head. "Go in the house."

Kit nodded, looking down. She could not look into his

eyes; it would have broken her heart to see his eyes. She was trembling. She pulled herself away from him. And started to open the door, then remembered. "Your coat," she said.

"Yes."

Kit took it off and helped him put it on in the narrow confines of the dooryard. It was still warm from her body.

She stretched up for a quick kiss then drew in a deep breath and opened the door. "Good night Daniel."

With his soul screaming No No No, Daniel said, "Good night Kit," and with his hand at the small of her back pushed her through the door.

Without looking back Kit closed the door. She wanted to turn back, to fling open the door, and pull Daniel in with her no matter how many flat mates were home, but she knew this was right and with tears running down her face she climbed the narrow stairs.

Daniel, feeling as though his insides had been pulled out, turned from the closed door, and stepped into the narrow street. His feet were heavy as anchors. The few steps back to the light where the creatures of the Commedia had cornered them, had tortured them, exhausted him. He leaned into the niche beneath the light to rest a moment before the next few steps. *God how could I?* He asked himself, but wasn't sure if he was asking how could he be in love with this young girl, or how could he have left this woman he loved so much.

Kit closed the door of her tiny room, and hung up her still sodden coat and hat. Her body trembled as though she was freezing, but it was the aching cold of loneliness. *How could I love this man?* She thought. *He is as old as my father.* But it didn't matter. His arms were warm and his heart was good and his kisses! Sweet God, his kisses made flames run through her body as no one else's ever had. But he was gone. He had done the right thing when she would have done anything to keep him with her, and it made her love him more.

The sound of the rain beating against her window called

Kit with thoughts of poor Daniel trudging toward the station in the downpour. She went to the window to close the shutters, but stopped with her hand on the latch. She could see the niche where she and Daniel had been trapped and in the haloed light of the street lamp beneath which Daniel had first kissed her, there was a man. He leaned against the wall beneath the lamp, his umbrella open but hanging useless in his hand. The look of him was defeated and hopeless. It made Kit want to cry out at his suffering, and it was only then that she realized it was Daniel.

Oh my poor darling! Kit thought and put her hand on the glass.

As if her thought had traveled to Daniel he turned and looked toward the lighted window. His hat brim shaded his eyes, but Kit knew that green gold stare recognized her, and the touch of those eyes against her was enough. Without another thought she was out her door and down the narrow stairs. She almost ran over her flat mate Marcy who said, "Steady on! What's up?" But Kit did not stop. She went out the street door leaving it open behind her and took the two steps across the dooryard. Daniel was there, a half step from the gate, coming toward the house. He stopped dead when he saw her and started to shake his head.

"I'm sorry Kit, I'm sorry," he said. "I couldn't go…"

Kit, soaked to the skin already, threw her arms around him and said, "No, you can't go! You can't. I need you too much."

"I tried to go—" Daniel was saying. "But I saw you in the window—"

Kit stopped his words with her kiss, and then said, "You can't go Daniel. I can't let you go. Please come back. I love you."

"But your roommates?"

"I don't care. I want you to make love to me."

Daniel's breath came in gasps and his heart was pounding

as though he had just run ten miles. *I can't, I can't, I can't!* He thought, but she was there and she wanted him and God knew he wanted her.

"Are you sure Kit? Are you really sure?"

For an answer she kissed him again.

Marcy was standing in the door with her mouth open watching them. When Kit and Daniel turned toward the door she said, "Gawd, you look like drowned cats! Come in, come in before we all have to swim for it."

Kit pushed past her, leading Daniel by the hand. They were both sopping.

"Who's this then?" Marcy asked, eyeing the trailing puddle they were leaving behind them.

"This is Daniel," Kit said. "Good night Marcy."

Marcy blinked at them as she watched them drip up the stairs. "Yes," she said at last. "Good night."

The room was small and seemed smaller when Daniel stepped into it, but they did not notice. They only had senses for one another as they undressed.

Daniel's manhood was straining with need and he was embarrassed by it at first, but when Kit stood naked before him, all shame disappeared. Her strawberry blond hair, all dripping wet strings, framed her face and draped down to her shoulders. Her breasts were pale globes of luminescence with coral confections for nipples. Her body was all lithe suppleness covered with silken flesh.

"My God Kit, you are so beautiful," he breathed.

She came into his arms then, pressing her nakedness against him as though trying to melt into his flesh. The maleness of him pressed against her belly and sent shivers of desire through her. She wanted to be one with him, to share the essence of him and have him take her essence into himself.

Daniel felt her need mingle with his own and he swept her up into his arms, took the two steps to the narrow bed and laid her gently down. He kissed her mouth and neck and breasts and belly and womanhood.

"Oh Daniel," she breathed. "I want you now. Please, please I want you now!"

He parted her legs and, with all the gentleness he could manage, entered her.

They moved together as though they had been lovers for all time. The rhythm was exact. They were locked together in that eternal moment when body, soul, and spirit meld, ceasing to be two and becoming one.

When they were spent Daniel started to withdraw, but Kit clamped her legs around him. "No. Please. Stay in me."

"All right," he breathed and kissed her yet again. He eased himself to the side, turning Kit with him so that they lay side by side with Kit's legs still around him. They filled the whole bed. Face to face, Daniel tried to find some shame, some regret within himself, but could only find love. He lifted his hand and stroked back the strands of hair that were still plastered across her face. "I love you Kit," he said. "I love you."

The words shot bolts of joy through her. She wanted to hear this man say them to her again and again for a hundred years, but in a second her joy gave way to truth. She put her hand against his mouth to stop the words. "Shhh. You mustn't. This can't be."

"Maybe not, but it is. I do. I have from the first instant I saw you."

"You must forget that. You must," she said, desperately wanting to hear him say it again.

"No way."

"But Amanda—"

"No. Don't. I can't talk about her now. I have to think what to do."

"Daniel, you mustn't hurt her. You loved her once."

"Please Kit, don't. Don't."

She could see the pain in his eyes and realized that it was more than just not wanting to hurt Amanda. There was still love for Amanda there.

"Daniel, you must keep this all to yourself. We can continue quietly and keep it from Amanda—"

"No! This is not some tawdry little screw. I love you Kit. I want you. I want to be with you always."

"—Or we can make this the end," she finished, and instantly regretted it for the anguish in Daniel's eyes was like that of an abandoned child.

Daniel pulled her face against his chest to stop her saying anything further. "No. This isn't going to be the end Kit. It isn't! I'll think of something. I'll figure something out."

Kit prayed silently that he would, but knew in her heart that this could only end in hurt for all concerned.

V

Amanda lay awake listening to the desert wind. It never seemed to be still, morning, noon, or night. In the dawn, it was a gentle breeze, but every afternoon it would rise and by dark, it would be blowing a gale that lifted the dust from the dry lakebeds and blew leaves and grass and bushes and trash cans down the streets. But the noise of the wind was a comfort to her just now. It concealed the sound of her weeping from Daniel who was sleeping beside her. She did not want to wake him. He seemed to be sleeping peacefully now and that was something which she cherished because it happened so seldom since Kit had—

She pulled her thoughts away from that, but they fell into another groove she did not really want to travel down again. Nevertheless her mind would not be bumped from this hated rut until it had run its course. The thoughts were scattered all over, but they all were bracketed by *WHY, WHY, WHY?*

Why had Daniel fallen in love with Kit, after twenty-eight years of loving only her? Why had it not just been some fling? A little roll in the hay that could be easily forgotten or forgiven if it ever came out? Why did he have to have the beautiful English girl so deeply in his heart that she tortured him even now, years later and half a world away?

But Amanda knew the answers. It couldn't have been just a casual fuck because that was not Daniel. He did not love or hate casually. His heart, if it was given over in love or hate, was committed. His heart had been committed to her for almost a lifetime. His love had freed her from a spiral of self destruction caused by her family, and, good times and bad he had been committed to her. When they didn't know where their next meal was coming from he had been committed to

63

her. He could have run away a thousand times, but he hadn't. He loved her and that meant good times and bad. That was why she stayed with him now for she did not love or hate casually either.

Amanda's family hated Daniel—had almost from the first day they set eyes on him—but he continued to go into their presence as often as she wanted because he loved her; because he would have done anything for her. She thought of all the times her family had insulted and scorned him, but he kept going back with her because he loved her then –loved her still. There were a few times, after her father and Daniel had nearly come to blows that she feared Daniel would leave her. She was not sure if she would have stayed in his place but he did. In spite of it all he stayed. That was the reason she stayed with him now despite Kit. Daniel had been Amanda's heart when she needed him desperately, and he needed her now in ways he had never needed her in their lives before, because he had also loved Kit. Oh God how he had loved Kit! And now that love was eating him alive.

When Amanda found out about Kit it was already too late; Amanda was just back from the dead herself, and in the joy of her husband's arms when she found out. She had hated Kit then, and felt guilty for hating anyone that Daniel had loved so. She was glad the English girl was dead and gone and could not take Daniel from her, but when she saw what Kit's death did to Daniel the hate for her doubled, and the guilt too. She wished Kit alive again so that she could fight her, so that... so that even if she lost Daniel to her he would not be in such agony. But she could not fight a ghost, and she could not heal her husband's heart. Only time and love might do that.

Might.

Daniel turned over, faced away from her and visibly tensed. He made a groaning sound. Amanda recognized it as part of the dream that kept coming back to haunt him. She wiped her eyes on the bed sheet and moved over against her husband. Letting him feel the warmth of her body, her touch. "Shh," she whispered. "Shhh. It's OK Danny. It's OK. You're here with me. It's OK."

But tonight her touch and her words weren't enough. The dream reeled on and Daniel couldn't wake from it until it finished and he sat stark up right screaming and fighting to reach Kit.

"Danny! Danny!" Amanda was shouting now to bring him awake. She ducked his swinging fists to throw her arms around him and pin his arms to his sides before he hurt himself or her.

"Danny, Wake up! Wake up! It's all right!"

The fighting rigidity went out of him then and he looked around the dark, wind haunted room for a moment, then he began to cry. Deep wracking sobs that tore at his guts and at Amanda's heart. "I should have been there, I should have been there," he wailed. "I could have stopped him!"

"No Danny you couldn't have. You couldn't have. It's all right. It's all right. I love you Danny. You're here and I love you."

At last Daniel stopped sobbing and lay down again. Amanda lay beside him and cradled him like she had seen him cradle their sons when they were small and afraid of dreams. She held him tight and whispered her love and protection until he went back to sleep, and silently prayed the dreams would not come back tonight.

***

Daniel and Kit woke early in Kit's tiny room. The sound of rain on cobblestones was a soothing whisper. Daniel brushed his lips against Kit's hair and drew in the perfume of her. He wanted always to remember the feel of her hair against his lips; the feel of his hands caressing her; the feel of her hand upon his chest. He stroked his hand down her side and she stirred and turned her face to him, smiling.

They made love again, slow and sweet, but when they lay

side by side afterward and Daniel once more whispered, "I love you," Kit knew what she must do. She pulled away from his arms and sat up.

"We can't Daniel," she said, putting as much iron in her tone as she could manage, hoping Daniel couldn't hear how fragile her resolve really was. "We cannot do this anymore. This must be the last— ever."

"But Kit…"

"No 'but Kit.' You say you love me, and God knows I love you, but for that very reason we must stop this. I love you enough to wish you happiness and peace in your life and we both know this will bring neither of those. For me it would be simpler, but it would wreck your family and destroy you. I cannot let that happen. I cannot. I love you too much to see you hurt because of me."

Daniel, smiling, reached out to her and stroked a finger down her naked breast. The nipple reacted, but Kit, with all the strength and love she could muster pulled away and slapped him as hard as she could.

Surprised and hurt Daniel pulled back and sat up. Anger flashed across his face and was gone. He lifted his hand to rub the place Kit had hit him.

Though her arm tingled from the jolt of the blow, and a voice in her mind screamed, *Kiss him Kiss him, Kiss him!* She clenched her teeth together and said, "Never, never, never do that again."

He breathed in and out several times still rubbing his cheek then said, "All right."

The words hurt her so much she thought she would cry out, but she kept her face stern.

Kit walked with him to the train station and even to the platform. There was only a moment before the train was to leave and Daniel turned to her. "Kit, I love you and there is no help for it, but if this is the way you want it then that's the way it will be." He quickly bent and kissed her, then jumped onto the moving train steps before she could react. His last sight was Kit standing on the platform looking waifish and beautiful in her too large brown tweed hat and voluminous raincoat. It was a memory that would haunt him forever.

Kit watched the train go out from under the station roof and into the mist of rain until she was sure Daniel could no longer see her then she took one step back and sat down on a concrete bench. She was shaking so hard she could not have stood another moment.

***

Daniel spent the rest of the week in furious, but silent activity. He spoke to almost no one, going about his needful business clenched into himself, trying to squeeze the great emptiness inside him into a more manageable corner. He wrote sloshy poetry like a love sick teenager, then laughed bitterly at it and threw it away.

He woke early on Sunday morning and thought about going to Venice to church, but he couldn't. He was afraid he would see Kit and not be able to stop himself from taking her in his arms. *This is going to be hard,* he thought and then thought, *this is going to be impossible,* but he didn't go to Venice.

At 10:30 the phone rang and startled him. It rang a second time and all the hope and desire and wishes and thoughts in him clouded up like dust on a desert wind. *Maybe it's Kit Maybe it's Kit Maybe it's Kit.* The thought paralyzed him with hope and dread.

The phone rang a third time and he came unstuck from the chair and ran to it. He picked it up and said "Pronto?"

"Oh you're there." It was Amanda. "I figured you would be in Venice. I was just going to leave a message on the machine."

Daniel swallowed hard and said, "No. I didn't feel like going down today."

"You all right, Danny? You sound kind of chokey. Are you sick?"

"No. I just woke up," he lied.

"Oh. OK. Now don't you be sick you hear me? I need you to take care of me."

"Are you sick?"

"No, just scared to death. That's why I called."

A twist of fear went through Daniel. "What's going on?"

"It's all over now. That's why I called to let you know that everything is OK before you see it on CNN. I'm OK and so is everybody else, but we're stuck here for a few days."

The twist of fear turned to a twist of guilt, because he had no idea what she was talking about. So self concerned had he been that he had not so much as turned on the TV or radio in days. "Where's here, what happened?" He asked.

"They shelled us," she said.

"What?" Daniel knew the words, but somehow they didn't connect to reality.

"As we were leaving Sarajevo somebody dropped a dozen or so mortar rounds on the runway. One of them came close enough to screw up an engine so we are stuck here for a few days."

"What the hell are you doing in Sarajevo? I thought you were in Spain? What happened to the exercise?"

"I can't talk about it. We were re-directed here."

"I thought the airport there was closed."

"It is, but C-130's don't really need anything except a flat enough place to land. That's why they sent us. They figured we could be in and out before anybody hardly noticed."

"Guess they were wrong."

"Yeah."

"Well, if the plane is broken how in hell are you going to get out of there?"

"We're working on it. I really don't know, but we'll get out somehow."

There was a clicking on the line. "Danny? Are you still there?"

"Yes."

"They're going to cut us off. I love you."

"Love you too," he answered automatically. "Keep your head down and your ass covered," he added. It used to be a joke he would say as he sent her off TDY, but suddenly it didn't seem so funny anymore.

"Pray for us Danny," she said, and the line went dead.

Daniel hung up the phone and went to the living room. He flipped on the TV to AFN, the Armed Forces Network, just in time to catch a reporter, an American Army staff sergeant, standing at the Sarajevo Airport. A C-130 stood in the background. There was fire foam still dripping from one engine and in puddles on the ground. Two trucks sat close by. Closed or not the airport seemed to have been able to summon crash trucks in time of need. *What would have happened if there hadn't been any crash trucks?* Daniel thought, and then shoved that thought away as hard as he could.

"None of the crew was hurt," the reporter said, "But the plane is grounded here for several days. IFOR, the combined European task force, is sweeping the area around the Airport to clear it of hidden mortar bunkers, but thus far their sweep has not turned up anything. This is..." Daniel stopped listening and flipped around to some of the Italian channels. Most of them were showing the usual Sunday morning fare. Masses from local churches and from Rome and family chat shows. One channel mentioned Sarajevo, but it was gone so fast that Daniel didn't catch it. His Italian was good, but not good enough to catch it on the fly. He had to concentrate on what was being said.

Finally he turned off the TV and went back to his office. He sat down in front of his computer and did what he often did when he needed to think. He wrote in the journal he had been keeping for thirty-five years.

What the hell am I doing? He wrote. *Amanda—I might have just lost Amanda to a random mortar shell and all I can think about is how much I need to see Kit. How horrible is that? How heartless? I have known and loved Amanda forever. She has been my friend and my lover and my life. We have sons together! I love her, but my heart hurts because Kit doesn't want to see me anymore. My heart hurts because Kit is more grown up than I am and knows that we can't do this, but if she called me this instant, I would be on my way out of this house so fast it would thunder behind me. I must be insane! Please God, help me. Please.*

Thursday morning Daniel woke early again. Dawn was just beginning to tint the snow on the Dolomite Alps. He felt as though he had just finished a day's work, but he didn't even try to go back to sleep. He had not really slept well since the night Kit had slept in his arms. He rose, put on shorts and a sweatshirt and went out for a run. Usually he would have reveled in the clear blue sky, the nip in the air, and the magnificent mountains, but today he could have been in the midst of a snowstorm and would not have noticed.

He stopped at the base gym two miles from home, and worked his way around the Nautilus circuit, but it wasn't enough. He still felt the longing need for Kit. It was an ache deeper than anything in his muscles, and the inability to ease the pain was causing a rage of frustration to build in him. He moved to the corner of the gym room where the speed bag and the heavy punching bag hung. His hands weren't wrapped nor did he take time to get a pair of gloves from the equipment room. Instead he moved into the heavy bag and began punching. Body blows to the bag—to the frustration of wanting and not being able to have. It was the story of his life. Wanting and hoping and working and praying and never having.

The shock of each punch jarred his arms and shoulders and the tape wrapped around the bag skinned his unprotected knuckles but he did not stop. The rage of frustration built and built as he punched so that he no longer felt the jarring. Nor did he feel the first split of the flesh of his knuckles.

The sound of a voice worked its way through his concentration and he realized that someone was calling his name. "…Dan! Stop it man! Your knuckles are all beat to shit! You're getting blood on the bag!"

Daniel stopped and looked up, not at first recognizing the huge black man who was calling his name. It was Chief Shabaz, but Daniel had been so distracted that he hadn't recognized the Chief.

"You should have at least got some gloves, man! You'll bust your hands all up. Look at that mess."

Daniel looked at the bloody mess that was his knuckles and smears of red on the tape of the bag. "Sorry, Chief," he said. "I had something to work off."

Shabaz ran his eyes over Dan. "You OK now?"

"Yeah. Yeah. I'm OK." But he wasn't. The consuming desire was still in his center.

"Come on. Let's get your knuckles patched up."

"No. It's OK Chief they aren't as bad as they look. I'll fix them when I get home."

Shabaz hesitated. "You sure, man?"

"Yeah. It's OK."

The Chief didn't really believe him but he let it go. "Well, all right," he said. "Next time get some gloves."

"Yeah, right. Sorry."

Shabaz looked him over one more time and turned away. Daniel headed for the door and began to run as soon as he was outside it. His knuckles burned and ached, but the pain wasn't enough to take his mind away. Kit's face was there.

Daniel came up the last quarter mile stretch with his head down, steam puffing from his mouth with each breath. He was exhausted, only able to concentrate on the few feet of road ahead of him. He turned in the gate and slowed to a shambling walk toward the front door.

"Daniel?"

His heart thudded and then soared. Kit was standing on the front steps, and no forbidding word or slap could have stopped him from throwing his arms around her and covering her face with kisses.

"I was afraid I had gotten the wrong house when no one answered the bell," she said, breathless, when he freed her mouth from his.

"How did you get here?" he asked, amazed.

"On the train. Then a Taxi from Pordenone. I didn't want to—"

"No. Don't say it. Don't. I love you and you had to come. Thank God, you had to come."

"I had to come," she said in a small voice. "I couldn't help it. I haven't slept in days. I haven't been worth anything in class. I'm sure my flat mates hate me by now, I have been so short with them."

"Doesn't matter. You are here now and—" Daniel suddenly realized that he was sweat soaked and probably smelled like a goat. He released her and stepped back. "I must stink to high heaven," he said. "Come in the house while I jump in the shower."

Kit bent to pick up her black knapsack and saw Daniel's bloody knuckles. She dropped the knapsack and took Daniel's left hand in hers. "What happened to your hands?"

Daniel snatched his hand away. "They're all right. You're here now and everything is all right again." He picked up her knapsack and they went in. Daniel put her on the couch in the living room, turned on the TV and went to the shower.

When he came out his hands were bandaged but there was no thought of the pain in them or the shaking of his exhausted muscles. Kit was still sitting on the couch, but she had her head in her hands. "What are we going to do Daniel?" She asked.

He sat beside her. "We are going to make love and not think about what to do after," he said and pulled her into his arms. "That is what we are going to do."

G.L. Helm

VI

Daniel woke. He had slept like a dead man for the first time in days. He turned on his side and reached across the bed. There was no one there and for a moment, there was a trickle of doubt in his chest. Had Kit's presence only been a dream? But then he knew it was not. He could feel her presence in the house. She was not lying beside him, but she was here.

He got out of bed, naked. The house was chilly and he looked for his robe but didn't find it. He settled for a pair of running shorts from the closet, pulled them on and went looking for Kit. He found her sitting at his desk bundled in his robe and sight of her took his breath away. She wasn't really small or fragile, but somehow she looked tiny and delicate as a Dresden figurine. Sunlight poured through the window and made her hair a red gold aura. She had reading glasses perched on her nose and was concentrating on the papers that lay on the desk before her. She had pulled the balled up poetry from the trashcan and smoothed them.

Daniel walked quietly behind her, gathered her hair in his hand, and then bent to kiss her neck. "Good morning Love," he said.

"Are these about me?" She asked.

"Yes."

She didn't say anything for so long that Daniel grew self-conscious and had to fill the silence.

"I'm sorry," he said. "It's what writers do when their hearts are breaking, we write poetry. Not usually as bad as that though."

"Bad? Daniel, these are wonderful."

"No they're not. They are sloshy adolescent junk. The only thing that makes them forgivable is that they are about you and you addled me enough to make me write them."

"May I have them?"

"Oh Lord," he groaned. "Kit my darling, they are trash, that's why I threw them away."

"I'd like to keep them all the same."

"I'll write some more. Better."

Kit shook her head and read aloud–

"Some say that heaven is beyond the sky.
But I think not.
Heaven is to rest when I am weary,
Eat when I hunger,
Drink when I thirst,
And have you beside me,
A moment longer than forever.

"That is so beautiful it breaks my heart," she said. "It is like a Cavalier poem from the Restoration"

"Not you too?" He said with mock disgust.

"What?"

"You think I am some kind of 17th century throwback. Amanda says..." He stopped. Amanda's name in his mouth had dried up all the other words.

Kit stood up and put her arms around him; her hands warm against his naked back, her face warm against his chest.

"She was on that plane that got shelled in Sarajevo, Kit," he said, his voice a brittle whisper.

Daniel felt the shock run through her. She looked up at him. "Is she hurt? What happened? I saw the report on the telly but I didn't think—"

"She's OK-- called me Sunday. Nobody got hurt, but the plane is unflyable. She wasn't supposed to be there. She was supposed to be in Spain."

Kit laid her head against Daniel's chest again and listened to the beat of his heart. There must be something more to say or do, she thought, but there was nothing so she just held him.

After a time Daniel kissed the top of her head and, with a

heartiness he didn't really feel said, "I think we need some breakfast. We can eat on the terrace if it isn't too cold. The mountains are beautiful."

"I'm afraid I'm no cook Daniel," she said ruefully.

"Of course not. You're an architect. I'm the cook. Would you like an omelet? Not sure what I have to put in it, but we'll manage something."

She leaned back in his arms to see if he was joking. In her world men did not cook, unless they did it professionally. "You're serious," she said.

"Of course," he said. "But if you're not hungry..." he put his lips against her forehead, "...we could always go back to bed."

"Does that mean you are still hungry?" She smiled and suddenly gave his chest a love bite.

"Hey! I better feed you before you get any more ideas," he said and kissed her again.

The Pentland's house had once been the carriage house of a fairly large estate. It had been remodeled and turned into a rental property when the flood of new personnel came into Aviano AFB. The carriage house was separated from the owner's house by a high hedge, and there were many trees around it so it was like a house in the woods though it was only a few steps from the main road into Aviano.

The terrace was really only a small porch off the kitchen, but there was room for a table and chairs and the view of the Alps was breathtaking. Daniel served ham and cheese omelets, toast, and orange slices. He was careful to make it an artistic presentation, complete with Blue Calico China and Silverware. He wanted to impress Kit and he did.

"I have never tasted an omelet so delicious.

"It's the air and the company," Daniel said, pleased. "I'm a pretty good cook, but not that good."

They sipped their coffee and watched the late morning sun

shift the colors of the mountains from dark green and rose to green variegate topped with ice cream white. "What is that Daniel?" Kit asked, pointing at a silver topped building a quarter of the way up the mountain.

"Chrome Dome," he answered

"Chrome Dome?"

"Well it is actually Madonna di Monte, but everybody around here calls it Chrome Dome because of the silver metal on the..."

"Dome?" She finished with wide-eyed false innocence.

"Exactly."

"Have you been inside?"

"Oh yes. The outside is the best part. Inside is pretty usual. They hired somebody to update the altar paintings and the guy was mediocre at best. The altar itself is quite pretty. Local marble and the tabernacle is beautiful. All carved wood. We can go up there later if you want. It's a beautiful view."

"I'd love to make some sketches of it."

"The view?"

"No, the church."

Daniel looked questioningly at her, and she smiled with a little of the imp in it. "With apologies to someone, it's what architectural students do. We sketch buildings."

"Ah," he said. "Hoist by my own petard. Whatever that means. What on earth made you want to become an architect?"

Kit's mouth did a cynical little twist and Daniel knew he had missed another sterling opportunity to keep his mouth shut.

"You mean because it is an odd profession for a girl?" She said bitterly.

"No. I didn't mean that at all. I just want to know about you. I want to know everything about you."

Kit blushed and looked away from his face. "I'm sorry," she said. "It's just that I have heard it ever since I started. *'Why would you want to deal with all that? You're such a pretty girl. It is SO difficult! All the mathematics. And you'll have to deal with construction tradesmen...'* My Da actually said that to me, and him a 'Construction Tradesman' himself. He's a stone mason."

"I would never ever say or even think that!" Daniel said, shaking his head. "Look at where I am and how I've lived my life. I'm the original woman's libber. I'm a camp follower! My wife is a Master Sergeant in the Air Force."

Daniel saw the flicker across Kit's eyes but didn't understand it at first, until he thought about what he had said. He had evoked Amanda's presence again. Without thinking he had called her forth like a ghost summoned by mention.

"I'm sorry Kit. I can't help it," he said. "She is here in this house and in my heart and there is going to be no getting around that. I have loved her for almost three decades. You don't put something like that out of your mind or out of your heart in a moment."

"In your heart, you said. Does that mean you still love her?"

The question was like an arrow shaft sticking into his chest. He drew several deep breaths and swallowed hard before he said, "Yes. I guess I do. But that doesn't mean I don't love you. It's just that Amanda and I have been through a lot together. You just can't throw that away."

"I saw the pictures of your sons in your office."

Daniel nodded. "Those are two of the visible results of things we have been through."

"This will hurt them won't it?"

He shrugged. "They are grown. They hardly keep in touch any more. If they even notice it will be a miracle."

"God this is horrible! I never pictured myself as a home wrecker, but here I am." She fixed her troubled blue eyes on Daniel's hazel ones. "It makes me wish we had never met."

"No," Daniel commanded. "No. If I died this second the only thing I would regret leaving is you. I love you.

Complicated as it makes our lives it is true, and I would not change it for anything on earth."

Kit and Daniel sat on a bench in front of Chrome Dome facing the church. Daniel usually sat on this bench facing the other way to look out over the Friulian countryside with its checkered fields and vineyards, but this time he watched Kit as she sketched. He could not take his eyes off her. She was like a talisman that warded off all fear and worry and guilt, but only as long as his eyes were on her. It wasn't sexual at all -- not that those thoughts did not pass his mind every few moments too, but this feeling he had was that Kit's presence set the world right again. Something had been wrong with his world for a long time, but she had somehow set it right.

Kit's eyes and hands were skillful. She made a half dozen sketches of the church as a whole and several of details around the church. The lines went down with draftsman's precision and at some point they stopped being just lines and took on life.

"Your drawings are better than the building," he said.

Without looking up from her drawing she said. "Again with apologies to someone, they are trash. I only do them to keep my hands and eyes sharp."

"They look pretty good to me. Bet you finish at the top of your class."

A cloud passed over Kit's face though the sky was clear blue. "I have to go back tonight," she said. "I have class tomorrow. I missed it last week..." She smiled ruefully and caressed his face. "I was distracted by something. The Professore was less than pleased."

"I'll drive you back anytime you say."

She looked from his face to her sketch and back to his face. "I don't want to go back Daniel. I want to stay here with you. I want to sleep beside you and eat omelets and draw and read your poetry and never go back."

Daniel took her hands in his and kissed them and said, "I want you to stay with me too, but that can't happen yet. There are problems to be worked out. When they are we will be together forever, I promise."

"Then take me back now. I have things to do to keep me busy until forever starts."

They stopped at the house then drove on to Venice. The drive was mostly silent with Kit sitting tight beside him. He felt like a silly teenager again, but would not have changed her position no matter if the whole world laughed.

Kit wouldn't let him park the car in the Piazzale Roma and walk her home. "It is hard enough to say goodbye here. Standing by my own door I'm not sure I could," she said.

"Your roomies would be shocked."

"Bugger 'em," she said and kissed him. She turned and hurried away before her resolve could weaken.

The house was cold as a crypt when Daniel got home, and not just because the weather had turned foggy and cold again. As usual when he was alone Daniel went to his office and turned on the computer. He wrote a few lines in his journal but gave it up as a bad job. There was nothing to say.

He glanced at the trashcan. It was empty. Kit had taken all the balled up poems home with her.

The telephone rang Saturday afternoon. Once more Daniel had been out running, beating his body relentlessly to try to keep Kit out of his mind. *If I can just exhaust myself maybe I can sleep,* he thought, but was still crushed when Kit wasn't standing on the porch waiting for him. He was soaked with sweat and breathing like a freight train when he picked up the phone.

"Pronto?"

"Pronto yourself..." Amanda said. "Come get me."

"Where are you?"

"Air Terminal. Come around back to the big doors."

"OK. I'll be there in half an hour."

"Half an hour? What'd ya gotta get rid of the floozies or something?"

Daniel's mouth suddenly went dry. "Yeah," he said after a moment, then half covered the receiver with his hand and shouted, "Cheez it girls it's my wife. Ya don't hafta go home, but ya can't stay here."

Amanda was laughing. "God, I love you Danny."

"You'll love me less if I pick you up smelling like this. I was just out running. I gotta jump in the shower. I'll see ya in half an hour."

Amanda was sitting on a pile of duffel bags in the cargo area. She looked pale and drawn and tired. Dark circles of weariness made her warm brown eyes like bottomless pits. Her usually razor creased BDU's were mussed and dirty. *She probably hasn't been out of them for days,* Daniel thought, and the thought hurt. *Here I have been worried so much about myself and 'Manda has been ducking mortar shells! What a bastard I am!*

Amanda looked up and saw him and the change was as if someone had flipped a switch. All the tired seemed to go out of her. Her cognac colored eyes sparkled and her smile could have melted glaciers.

"'Bout time you got here!" She said, throwing herself into his arms and kissing him firmly. It made Daniel's knees go weak and caused a flood of love to cascade through him. A lifetime of loving this woman, of fighting with her and beside her, of struggling to raise two sons, of support for his stupid dreams of writing books; and he was betraying it. Preparing to throw it all away.

"Are you all right, 'Manda?" He asked, holding her back from him to look at her. "You didn't get hurt any kind of way?"

"Only my pride," she said. "Danny, I was so scared I wet my pants."

He waited a beat for the rest of the joke, but it didn't come. Her face told him there was no laugh at the end of this story. "And I'm so tired..." The energy was draining out of her fast. "The flight was a bastard. If I'd had anything to eat within twelve hours I would have ralphed it all up, but I didn't so I only had the dry heaves almost from Sarajevo out."

"What the Hell were you doing in Sarajevo anyway?"

"Delivering a Dialysis machine."

Daniel blinked, shook his head, and said, "Let's go home. Tell me about it later. You want to stop at MARIO'S and get something to eat?"

"I want you to take me home and make me some pomodoro while I take a shower and then I want you to screw my brains out. Being close to explosions has a strange effect on me."

Daniel blinked again, tried to swallow the mouthful of ashes that had suddenly appeared on his tongue and smiled. "OK," was all he managed to say.

Amanda ate like a starved orphan, talking around every bite. "We got a call from the wing that asked if we could jump to Naples and pick up this Dialysis machine and take it into Sarajevo. Apparently there was only one in the whole damn country and some fool dropped a rocket on it. I couldn't believe they would shell a hospital, but they did."

"Doesn't surprise me in the least. War between Christians and Muslims has been simmering for a thousand years. Communist Yugoslavia just interrupted it for a while."

"Well, anyway, there were like a hundred people that needed it after operations, but they couldn't be dialyzed because of the machine being blown up. So some American Navy Surgeon who is working with the Med-Services for IFOR hears about this and some of the patients are kids so he gets on the horn to somebody who says 'Yeah we got a portable one here in the basement if you can come and get it.'

"So this starts the whole chain of events. You know how it goes. A bunch of brass sees a chance to get a little good guy polishing and we wind up hopping to Naples to deliver a kidney machine to Sarajevo."

"But why you guys?" Daniel said. He had asked this same question five or six times in the last hour and had yet to get a satisfactory answer.

Amanda shrugged with another mouthful of spaghetti hanging on her fork. "This is so good, Baby. God I missed you."

"Amanda!"

"We were available. The Exercise was pretty much a bust and you know they don't leave empty C-130's just clanking around, especially when there is some good publicity to be had."

"But why you?" Daniel reached across the table and poked her in the chest. "In case you didn't know it you're still a woman and women aren't supposed to go into combat situations..."

"Tell that to the kids in Iraq," she said.

Daniel shook his head. "This wasn't Iraq. Why were you there?"

"It's a different world than when we came in, Danny. A different world all together."

Daniel shook his head, still not satisfied with her answer. "We created a monster, Amanda. Women going to war! American Air Force planes flying mercy runs and getting shot at doing it."

"You should have seen it! When the C-130 came in to get us they did a combat off and on load. They were shoving the pallets with the replacement engine for the other bird out the back door while the plane was still moving and we hooked cables to our baggage pallet and drug it up the second the plane

84

stopped. Total time on the ground was maybe two minutes. It was like something out of Vietnam newsreels. I was so proud of those guys!"

And then it hit him.

"You volunteered to go, didn't you?" He said.

The fork full of spaghetti stopped half way to her mouth and her face reddened.

"And I'll bet you had to scream and threaten to make them let you go didn't you?"

"No."

"You could have gotten yourself killed!"

A vagrant thought raced across Daniel's mind. *What if that mortar had hit a fuel tank? And then, How much simpler..."* but he cut that one off before it was born. He would not think it. He would not think it!

"Danny, leave it alone OK? It was part of the job," she said.

"The Job? Again with the Job?"

"Danny!" She tried to pass it off lightly. "You knew the job was dangerous when you took it, right?"

"You didn't have to take it, but you did as you damn pleased again just like always without a thought for me or the boys! Just once I wish you would choose me over the damn Air Force." Daniel stood up and walked out of the kitchen.

After a little while Amanda stood and followed him. She found him sitting in front of the computer again. The screen was blank.

"I'm sorry Danny," she said. "I just had to go."

"No you didn't."

She put her hands on his shoulders. "I won't volunteer again I promise."

He reached up and put his hands on hers. "Go back and eat your spaghetti," he said.

At last Amanda leaned back and patted her tummy like

Shirley Temple. "I eat it all up," she said.

Daniel ran his eyes over her. He was still angry with her, but he was glad she was alive. She still looked tired, but much better than a couple of hours ago. She was in her long pink flannel housecoat and ratty old fuzzy slippers. Her hair, still damp from being washed, was wrapped in a blue towel. She was beautiful. She was alive and beautiful and he loved her.

"That look you got in your eyes," Amanda said. "That's a nice look, that look."

He knew what was coming and it made the acid in his stomach start churning. "You look awfully tired, babe. We can wait until tomorrow," he said.

"Maybe you can." She stood up, leaving her dirty plate and silverware where they lay on the table. "Come along with me, my boy. I want to show you something." She took his hand and led him from the kitchen down the hall to the bedroom. She had turned the bed down earlier and without a word she skinned out of her housecoat and towel and lay naked on the bed. She crooked a finger at him.

Always before, this sort of game had been wonderful. Daniel had loved it when Amanda played the wanton. It had taken years to convince her that sometimes he liked it when she took charge; now he almost wanted to turn and run. She lay, outstretched, small breasts pointed up still, despite having suckled two babies. Her belly wasn't board flat like it had been when she was eighteen, but the curve of it had a voluptuous quality that he had found pleasing. Her legs were still long and strong, though not the velvet over steel they had once been.

Looking at her he felt the first tingles of arousal behind his manhood and thought, *maybe I can do this. Just concentrate on Amanda.*

He went to her and began kissing her lips and neck, at the same time gently stroking his fingertips down her body.

Amanda, with the passionate urgency of one who has been close to death, but has survived, kissed harder and harder and grasped harder with arms and legs and hands. "Now Danny, now. Take me now!" She begged/commanded.

Daniel, concentrating on the silkiness of her skin, on the hardness of her nipples, on the warmth of her thighs, moved himself over her and put himself into her. He began the slow deep rhythm that usually brought him to the end quickly, but tonight it was no good. For the first time in almost thirty years, Daniel could not maintain his erection.

At last he gave up trying and rolled off. He covered his eyes with his arm. "I'm sorry 'Manda. I don't know what's wrong," he lied.

Amanda turned and put her arm and leg over him. Protective. "It's OK babe. I just rushed you before you were ready. It's OK."

"Maybe tomorrow. You need to rest anyway."

As if on cue she yawned against his shoulder. "I am whupped," she said. "Set the clock though. I want to go down to church tomorrow. I mean I *really* want to go down to church tomorrow. I never prayed so hard in my life as when those rounds were falling around us. Time to do a little God thanking I think. Sleep tight."

Daniel turned and kissed her forehead. "Sleep tight," he said, but she was already sleeping.

VII

Desert sun-dazzle made Amanda almost blind when she came in. She had come in from work and stopped to look at her roses before coming into the house. She was inordinately proud of her roses. She pampered and watered and clipped them like a Bonsai Master tending his precious trees, fighting back the desert to maintain her little oasis. Hers were the best, or nearly the best at Edwards. No sun or wind blasted petal ever stayed on Amanda Pentland's roses more than a couple of hours before she nipped it off, but the half dozen she had clipped off today weren't at all blasted or withered. They were perfect, half opened past the bud stage, but not full blown.

"Hello," she called as she came in the kitchen door.

"Hello," Daniel answered from the back of the house.

Amanda put the roses in one of her crystal vases and added some water then headed back to show Daniel. She went to the master bedroom, but didn't find him. "Danny where are you?"

"I'm in here," he answered.

The simple statement sent a shiver down her back despite the 100-degree temperature. It had come from the office. Daniel had hardly gone into the office since they had been at Edwards. They had moved the big desk from storage and set it up like a good working office with writing desk space as well as space for the computer, but Daniel had not sat at the desk for more than the moments it took to do the house business, and had not turned on the computer at all so far as she knew. He had not written a word in more than two years, not on the computer, not with pen, or pencil, or crayon. Until now.

Amanda stepped into the office. Danny was sitting before the computer screen, which had lines of words on it. He turned to her when she came in.

"What beautiful roses," he said.

"It's like the bushes exploded! They are practically groaning under the weight of roses."

"Did you have a good day?"

"Not bad. The usual. Everybody above Master Sergeant is an idiot and God help the Air Force, the civilians are taking over everything. The inmates are running the asylum." Amanda wanted those last few words back as soon as they were out of her mouth, but Daniel didn't seem to notice.

She wanted to ask what he was working on, but didn't want to break whatever relieving spell had fallen on her husband with her curiosity, so she left after a little more chitchat. An hour or so later Daniel came out smiling and they had a pleasant evening.

Another dream of Kit started an hour or so after they went to bed, but the desert wind banged the window shade and the noise woke Daniel before the nightmare could finish unreeling. He jolted awake and when he realized he was awake he lay still for a moment to see if he had wakened Amanda, but her breathing continued the long slow drafts of sleep. He lay still on the bed for a time, listening to the wind bang the shade. He didn't try to go back to sleep for fear the rest of the dream would continue and leave him screaming and fighting, trying to reach Kit. It usually did. *At least it wasn't Dr Pest and the coffin,* he thought. That one was the worst.

This dream had been still in the good part when the wind woke him. He was stretched out in the grass and Kit seated beside him. They rested on a grassy patch beside Lake Barcis, the bluest blue alpine lake in the world, and Kit concentrated on the watercolor she was making of the scene.

Daniel could hardly take his eyes off her. In life he had felt as though a part of him was missing when she was out of his sight. In this dream it was the same, only there was a dread that had not been there when he and Kit had made that trip to

Lake Barcis.

Kit had been a little the worse for wear that day. The two of them had ridden to the alpine tarn on bicycles and Kit's soft strawberry blond hair was clumped together in sweaty knots. The joy of lying beside her had made his soul ache with such longing then that he had stretched up his hand to stroke her damp hair and she had smiled at his touch. Remembrance of that day made the ache of longing that had been locked away return.

That ache was never far from him. Tears waited just below the surface of his consciousness most of the time. If he saw a woman with sapphire blue eyes or light cinnamon colored hair it made his heart leap until reality set in again. God forbid that he should hear a woman with an English accent say "Super!" That one word could take all the strength out of him and reduce him to a blubbering puddle no matter where he was.

But at least the desert wind had awakened him while he was still in the good part of the dream—the good part of his life. The part before London and Newcastle. Before...

"You OK, Danny?" Amanda asked. Something had wakened her. She was more attuned to him now-a-days. Just a small change in his breathing would bring her awake. She stretched out her hand toward him but didn't touch him.

"Yeah, I'm OK. Go back to sleep."

Daniel felt Amanda's eyes sweep over him in the dark. He didn't need to see the hurt and worry in them. Her gaze was hot as sunrays.

"Kit again?" She asked.

"No," he lied. "Just the wind."

Amanda knew it was a lie, but she didn't say anything about it, just rolled over with her back toward her husband and pretended to go back to sleep.

At last Daniel got up, pulled on some gym shorts and went out to the patio. He wished for a cigarette, or his pipe, but it was a fleeting wish. He hadn't smoked in years, but there were still times, especially on these midnight sojourns, that he wished he hadn't quit. Little white happy pills were no substitute for the feeling of tobacco smoke in the lungs. It was just another example of getting what you want only to have it turn out to be something you never intended it to be. Stop smoking so you can live an extra twenty years, only to have each of those extra years seem a hundred years long because you don't have the comfort of tobacco.

Daniel sat on the patio in the desert night and remembered his marriage vows. They echoed around his mind and bound him with chains stronger than steel. They ran down grooves worn to deep ruts over the last year. He hated himself for taking them so long ago, and he hated himself for breaking them with Kit.

If I had not made those vows, he thought for the ten thousandth time.

If he could have casually disregarded them like so many from his generation had, maybe he wouldn't be sitting on a patio listening to the desert wind, loving Kit, but still loving Amanda... Cherishing memories of Kit even as he tried to shove thoughts of her away before they devoured him.

Maybe Kit would still be alive.

Maybe.

***

Daniel did everything he could to avoid going to St. George's church the morning after Amanda returned from Sarajevo. He turned off the alarm clock so that Amanda would not wake. He lay still and quiet in bed though he was awake, so as not to wake her, but the gods had other ideas. Amanda woke just before the alarm should have gone off and, without a thought rolled over, kissed Daniel to wake him and headed for the shower.

Daniel stayed in bed and pretended to have fallen back asleep, but when Amanda came out of the shower looking delicious in her nakedness she said, "Come on sleepy head. Get your cute little ass up and showered. Time's wasting." Then she went to the kitchen to make coffee.

She came back to find Daniel still in bed and said, a little more forcefully, "Don't you dare mess around and make us miss the train. So help me I'll make you drive us all the way down there and I know how much you hate that."

"OK, OK. I'm up," he said and rolled out of bed.

Daniel continued with his usual routine of shaving and showering and having a cup of coffee but tried to go slow. It didn't help. Amanda was right there prodding and chivvying him along, patience wearing thinner moment by moment.

At last they were in the car heading for the Pordenone train station, but when they reached the Air Force base Daniel turned left to go through the gate.

"What are you doing?" Amanda said, exasperated.

"I'm gonna get a Sunday Stars and Stripes, just like always."

"Daniel, We're Late!"

"Don't worry about it."

He stopped at the Shoppette, picked up the paper, cursed the fact that there was no waiting line, and was back in the car quickly.

"OK. Let's go!" Amanda said with comically clenched teeth. "I don't know why I love you! You try my patience sometimes!"

"Sorry," he answered and drove on to the train station in Pordenone. They made it with minutes to spare.

The train pulled into Santa Lucia and the acid in Daniel's stomach went from a simmer to a slow boil of dread, but at the same time his heart was laughing and dancing in his chest. Every beat said KIT KIT KIT KIT KIT.

The day was cold, clear, and beautiful. Even at eight thirty on a Sunday morning the streets around the station were thronged with people, many in full Carnival costume. It was exciting and Amanda reacted to it like a delighted little girl, her head turning and turning, and her eyes wide. She hung onto Daniel's hand as they walked across the Grand Canal Bridge almost skipping with delight.

They walked quickly down the streets, past the park, over the bridge, to the left, along the small canal, crossing and crossing and crossing the transverse canals. Sixteen bridges large and small they crossed between Santa Lucia and Campo San Vio where St. George's stood. They stopped at the pasticceria (pastry shop) just past Campo Santa Margherita and had cappuccino and brioche, the sticky sweet apricot jam filled croissant that was the universal breakfast of Italy.

And then they were there, outside the half open bronze doors of St. George's with baroque organ music wafting out to them. Amanda pulled at Daniel's hand and stopped him for moment before they went in. "I love this Danny" she said looking around the small Campo. "I love this place." She stretched up a little and kissed him. "And I love you, no matter how patience trying you are." She wiped lipstick from his mouth and smiled. The smile and the thought stabbed Daniel's heart.

They went in.

Daniel glanced around the sanctuary. There were a few people already sitting, but Kit was not among them. He did not know whether to heave a sigh of relief or cry out in pain.

The church was icebox cold again. The radiators clanked and hissed, but everyone was still bundled in overcoats. Tiny clouds of steam rose from their breaths.

Amanda and Daniel went to their usual place on the left side behind the British Consul, knelt, and made the sign of the cross to prepare themselves for the service. Amanda, head bowed, eyes closed, hands folded, silently prayed, *Thank you dear God that I am alive and able to come to this beautiful place to pray.*

Daniel, head bowed, eyes closed, hands folded prayed, *"Dear God what am I going to do? I love them both and I don't want to hurt either of them. Help me God. Please. Have mercy on me."*

***

Kit woke and rose. She followed her usual Sunday morning routine without thought. In her mind hopes and desires and thoughts turned over and over and all concerned Daniel Pentland. Her body hungered for him even now. She wanted his kiss and his touch, and his heart beating against her breast, but, more than that, she wanted his essence; that aura which was Daniel. She wanted them to be together, no matter what.

Outside the door of St. George's she stopped and sent a little prayer to God. *Please let him come today. It will hurt me to see him, but please let me see him.* And God acknowledged that prayer. Inside, in the pew on the left directly behind the British Consul Daniel knelt, his wife beside him.

A soft step in the aisle brought Daniel's eyes open and his heart leaped even as his belly clenched. Kit stood beside the pew, stained glass tinted sunlight playing on her face. "May I sit here?" She asked.

Oh God! Please! Daniel's mind cried, but he was not sure if he meant Please let her sit here or Please don't.

"Good Morning Kit," Amanda whispered. "Sure. Sit down. Scoot down Danny."

Daniel could feel the throb of his pounding heart all the way to his finger tips. For a moment he could not get enough air, but he inched over and Kit knelt beside him. She made the sign of the cross, bowed her head, folded her hands and prayed silently, *Thank you Father, Thank you. Please help us. Please help me. I love him so much.* She leaned against him a little, touching him from shoulder to knee.

Kit's perfume made his head spin. He remembered how it

95

felt to bury his face in the heaven of her hair, how she felt in his arms, but he kept his hands folded, his eyes closed and his head down.

The sanctuary bell rang and they stood. Canon Doyle came down the aisle to begin the service.

Daniel dropped his right hand to his side and found Kit's hand waiting for it, just like he hoped it would be. He squeezed her fingers and wanted to bring them to his lips so much he could feel the muscles of his arm flex in preparation to do so, but he contained himself, content with the pressure Kit returned him.

Amanda noticed the tension in Daniel. He seemed clenched into himself, but it was not the usual closed self he presented. He seemed to be in pain. "Are you OK Danny?" She asked.

"I'm all right. I don't feel very well though. I'm cold."

That's why he was so draggy this morning, Amanda thought. *The poor thing is sick.*

The service continued through hymns, collect, prayers, homily, collection, Eucharist, and recession. Daniel was exhausted. Church was usually a solace. Today it was a trial.

At last it was finished. The small crowd milled around at the back of the sanctuary talking to Canon Doyle and to one another. Kit stayed as close to Daniel as she could without being too obvious about it.

Amanda asked Daniel, "Are you OK Sweet?"

Daniel saw a chance to end this right then. All he had to say was, No. I'm not OK can we go home now, but that would mean leaving Kit and he could not do that. Not now, perhaps not ever. Confession hung right at the back of his throat and almost gagged him. He wanted to tell Amanda; he wanted to take Kit in his arms; he wanted to run far and fast away from this pain, but he didn't.

"I'm OK. Let's go get some coffee." he said.

Amanda smiled. "Are you coming too Kit?" she asked. The small jealousy of weeks before was gone, washed away by joy of life and of having Daniel, sick or well, holding her hand.

"If you don't mind?" Kit answered.

"Heavens no. Come along."

In the pub they ordered coffee and Daniel ordered himself a cognac. "Little early for that isn't it?" Amanda asked.

"I'm cold. 'Coffee for the hands, cognac for the feet'" he quoted.

"I don't like the taste of cognac," Kit volunteered.

"Me either," Amanda agreed.

"But it does build a fire in your belly if you're cold." Memory of Kit, drenched, crying, and shivering as she sipped cognac and made faces at the taste crossed his mind.

"So how have you been Kit?" Amanda asked.

Without missing a beat Kit answered, "Super."

Amanda and Kit chattered on about nothing at all for half an hour with Daniel adding an occasional word, but for the most part he just listened and watched. The women seemed to get along wonderfully. They smiled and laughed and ignored him. Daniel was astonished. They could be friends, he thought. Impossible ideas of some sort of polygamous marriage raced round his brain, but the cynical part of him put thoughts of having ones cake and eating it too close on their heels.

People from church drifted in and out of the Pub. Canon Doyle and his wife Elizabeth arrived. It took them longer because he had to change from vestments to clothes and his wife, Elizabeth, could not move too fast. She was a small woman, made smaller by being hunched over. She had severe arthritis, and the cold damp weather made her almost an invalid. She seldom came out of the house and when she did she walked with two canes. She was the perfect model of a crone, except that her face made that a lie. It was effervescent like a young girl's. Though she was often in pain her mouth was usually turned up in a smile.

Daniel stood when the Doyle's came up to the table. "Good morning, Elizabeth," he said, bowing a little. He did it unawares.

"Good Morning dear Daniel," the old woman answered. Her eyes caressed Daniel's face and she stretched up a little to give and receive the proper Italian greeting of a kiss on both cheeks.

Daniel and Canon Doyle helped her to a seat and took her sticks. Her eyes, jet black and piercing, sharpened as they looked into Daniel's. "What is the matter Daniel? You do not look well. Something is troubling you."

Daniel swallowed hard. This old woman had read him as though there was a sign around his neck. "I guess I am still a little shook about Amanda's getting shelled in Sarajevo," he lied.

"You were on that plane Amanda?" Canon Doyle asked, shocked. "It was all over the news."

"Yes sir," she answered.

"That must have been terrifying," Kit said.

"It had its moments," Amanda said.

Elizabeth's eyes swept over the group and came back to rest on Daniel's face. "Yes, I can see how you might be still a little shaken by that. But it is over now. Amanda is safe."

"What on earth were you doing in Sarajevo?" Canon Doyle asked.

Amanda explained about the kidney machine and the escape. "Good heavens!" Doyle said, "We are certainly happy to see you back safe and sound."

They chatted on for a little. Elizabeth seldom looked directly at Daniel, but when she did he could feel the scorch of her questioning eyes. *The guilty flee when no man pursueth,* he thought with a bitter mental laugh.

At last Canon Doyle said, "Are you staying for lunch?"

They all were.

"Perhaps we'll just go to I Gondolieri today. I don't believe Elizabeth is up for the walk to San Stefano," Doyle said and they agreed.

Conversation continued during lunch. It was one of the reasons Amanda and Daniel continued to come all the way to Venice for church, and, as usual, it was lively and witty and fun, but today Daniel couldn't enjoy it. He had hoped to get a moment alone with Kit, but by the time the group got the bill and did the divvying up and started their goodbyes it hadn't happened.

The last thing before they all parted, Elizabeth took Daniel by the lapel and said. "Why don't you come down and see me Daniel. Tell me more about what you are writing. The weather has been so terrible that I have hardly been out of the house. I would appreciate a visitor."

Amanda heard her. "Elizabeth, I will see that he comes down soon. Perhaps I'll be able to come too," Amanda promised.

Elizabeth ran her eyes over them and smiled. "That would be wonderful. I'll look forward to it."

Later, on the train, Daniel said, "I think I'll go back and visit Elizabeth tomorrow."

"Oh. But I can't go tomorrow," Amanda said.

"That's all right. We can go together a little later. She will be glad to get two visits instead of one."

"I guess that's true. I really feel sorry for her. "

"Me too. She is sharp though. Got a mind like a theologian."

Amanda laughed. "She is quick and she's in love with you, you know."

"You think?"

"Absolutely."

Daniel wiggled his eyebrows and in his best Charles Boyer accent said, "But of course. All the women are drawn to Pepy

Lemoco."

Amanda laughed again. "And if she were twenty years younger I would have to worry about her, wouldn't I?"

"Nah. Now if she were forty years younger," Daniel said and tried to smile.

"Why you dirty old man!" She pinched him in the side.

Dirty old man, Daniel thought. *Guess that about covers it.*

VIII

Daniel hardly slept. The anticipation of seeing Kit kept his nerves pulled tight as banjo strings. He was like a child at Christmas. Amanda had wanted to make love. She had started the overtures on the train, but Daniel ducked into his office as soon as they were home and hid out by pecking away at the computer until it was too late. He wanted to hold her and pet her, but was sure any love making was doomed from the start. He still loved her, was glad she was alive but, no matter how much his mind told him this failure was stupid, that men cheat on their wives all the time and kept having sex with them, his heart wouldn't let him be so false.

The next morning rain was threatening again. "Maybe you better put this off," Amanda said.

"Nah. I'll take my umbrella."

Amanda studied her husband. Something was wrong. She could see it. And it was more than just his lack of desire for her. That was bad enough, but it hadn't worried her as much as it seemed to have worried Daniel. She had read that couples go through this kind of thing and thought they had been very lucky never to have had any problems before. But there was something more.

The idea that Daniel was having an affair crossed her mind, but was discarded with the thought, *in all these years that I have been going away and leaving him alone for weeks, sometimes months at a time he has never strayed so far as I know. Why would he start now?* Still, the question kept buzzing around her mind. *I'll just watch and be patient for a while* she thought.

Amanda drove Daniel to the train station before she went to work. As he was getting out of the car he said, "I have no idea when I'll get back 'Manda. The streets and the trains are probably gonna be jammed. I'll either call or grab a cab."

"Looks like it's gonna pour any second. Are you sure you want to do this?"

"It'll be all right," he said and closed the door.

Amanda shouted, "Hey, Hey," and leaned over to knock on the window. Daniel turned back and opened the door.

"You are not going to get away without kissing me goodbye," she said. "I want you to remember to come home."

Daniel smiled ruefully. "Sorry." He leaned in and kissed her offered mouth. Amanda lifted a hand and touched his face.

"I love you Danny," she said.

"Love you too," he echoed. It was a throw away line, said a thousand times without thought. "Drive careful." He closed the door and turned into the station doors.

Amanda waited a moment then drove off.

Daniel glanced back in time to see Amanda drive off. He turned to the bank of telephones and dropped a thousand Lira coin into one and dialed, hoping to catch Kit before she left for class.

No such luck. The phone rang a long time and just as he was about to hang up someone picked up. "Pronto," they said. The voice was female and English.

"Kit? Is that you?" he asked.

"No, this is Marcy. Kit isn't in. She's gone to class."

His heart sank. "When will she be back?"

"Don't know."

Daniel thought for so long that Marcy said, "Are you still there?"

"Yes, I'm here. Look. Could you leave a message for her?"

"Yeah sure."

"OK. Tell her that Daniel called and that he's coming into Venice. Ask her to meet him at Bar Redemptor at noon."

"I doubt she'll be able to be there at noon," Marcy said. "I think her class this morning runs until 12:30."

"OK. Make it One o'clock."

"All Right. Kit is to meet Daniel at one in Bar Redemptor. I'll leave the note here by the blower, but if she doesn't come back here right after class she might not see it until tonight."

"Do you see her during the day?"

"Sometimes."

"If you see her today will you give her the message?"

"If I see her."

"Thank you."

"Prego," she answered and hung up the phone.

Daniel hung up and had to run for his train. He found a seat in one of the compartments, but it was clear that this was not going to be a pleasant trip. Leave aside the fact that worry about Kit not getting his message was eating holes in his guts, the train was near full of rollicking people on their way to Venice to join in the Carnival celebrations. And it could only get worse as they moved toward Santa Lucia. Half the passengers were already drunk on wine at 7:30 in the morning and the other half were drunk on the celebration of the season. Singing and shouting and laughing were everywhere. Except that he hated being drunk or being around drunks Daniel almost envied these revelers.

Sitting on the train being steadily jammed tighter and tighter into his corner as more revelers piled aboard, Daniel began to wonder if this whole idea was not snake bit from the beginning. *Just another little chuckle for the gods,* he thought cynically. *See the fool trying to be somewhere he shouldn't and watch us throw comic road blocks in his way.*

By the time the train pulled into Santa Lucia the party was at full roar, with people hanging out the windows and doors like some circus train full of clowns. *All we need is elephant poop to make it perfect,* Daniel thought, as he used the ferule of his umbrella to pry his way down the train's aisle.

The platform was no better. There was hardly room to

turn around and the distance from platform to the station's front steps which usually took a couple of minutes to cross now took ten, and cost a hundred bumps and pushes. The Santa Lucia Station Bridge across the Grand Canal was something out of Hieronymus Bosch with ten thousand masked figures moving in lock step across it to the boiling human cauldron of the Fondamenta San Simone Piccolo.

Still a week until Fat Tuesday, Daniel thought. *What is it going to be like on Mardi Gras?*

At last, after almost forty five minutes of elbowing and prying his way through the mob Daniel reached the relative quiet of the streets around San Pantalone. He was thankful above all things that he did not have to go near Piazza San Marco. That would have been like the train station multiplied by a hundred. When he reached the Gallerie Accademia he stopped for a moment, considering whether to go on to Bar Redemptor, or to make a real attempt to visit Elizabeth. He looked at his watch. It was after ten o'clock. Three hours until Kit would come. *If she comes,* his doubt demon whispered.

He turned and walked straight down the Rio Foscarini to the Zattere ai Gesuati, turned left and went down to the old Salt warehouse. There he turned left again and a little way up he turned right into the alley where the Doyle's apartment was located. He rang the bell and waited. He was about to ring again when he heard footsteps coming down the stairs inside and Canon Doyle opened the door.

"Daniel," the old man said, opening his arms and smiling broadly. The smile faded a little when he saw that Amanda was not with him. "I wondered if you would come back today. Come in, Come in. Elizabeth will be so glad to see you." He stepped back and let Daniel come into the foyer.

"Amanda had to work", Daniel explained, taking off his coat and hat and putting his umbrella in the stand. "We'll try to come back in a couple of days."

"That would be wonderful, but perhaps you should wait

until after Carnival," Doyle said and started up the stairs.

"Tell me about it," Daniel said. "The train was surreal and the station was worse."

"It is going to be even worse before it gets better. Thank God we live in nice quiet Dorso Duro."

The heat of the house increased toward oven like as they went up the second flight of stairs. Not for the first time Daniel wondered why the Doyle's stayed in this house. To love Venice was one thing, but for Elizabeth to hobble up and down these stairs was crazy. But he hadn't ever asked.

Elizabeth was seated in her large wing backed chair. The room was baking hot, but she had a shawl draped over her shoulders and an afghan over her lap.

"Daniel," she said smiling. Her eyes twinkled. "I wondered if it was you when I heard the bell."

Daniel went to her, bent and kissed her on both cheeks. "And how are you doing today?" he asked.

"Well. I am doing very well now. Buoyed up by your visit."

"Flatterer," he said and grinned as he sat down.

Father Doyle said, "If you'll excuse me Daniel I must go back to my office. I'm working on a speech in Italian for tonight. Since I am the only non-Roman priest in Venice I get called on for everything Ecumenical. Rather like the Catholic Bishop's trained monkey," he laughed.

"Better you than me," Daniel said, laughing with him.

Doyle went out and left the two alone. After a moment Elizabeth said, "I am always happy to have visitors Daniel, but I have the feeling that I am not the real reason you fought your way through the Carnival siege."

Daniel blinked a couple of times and grinned, abashed. "Am I really that transparent?"

"No," she smiled. "But almost."

They sat looking at one another for a long while. Elizabeth was patient, waiting to see where Daniel wished to

105

take this visit.

The heat of the room was growing more oppressive to Daniel moment by moment. He was beginning to sweat.

"Elizabeth, did you ever feel like your life wasn't really your own? That God or somebody was moving you around for laughs, like a character in some divine novel?"

She nodded. "Destiny. It is something that every culture wrestles with. Our scriptures give mixed messages about it." She paused, but Daniel didn't add anything so she said, "It can also be a convenient scape goat for free will gone wrong."

"I suppose it can," he said.

Suddenly Daniel felt the upwelling need to tell someone about Kit. He tried to bite the words off, but they bashed against the backs of his teeth like battering rams until they freed themselves. "I'm in trouble Elizabeth," he said. "I am in so much trouble. It's Kit Marlowe. I'm afraid I have fallen in love with her."

Elizabeth nodded. "And she is in love with you too." It was not a question. "I saw yesterday."

"Oh God," Daniel said. He brought his hand up to rub at his forehead, half hiding behind the gesture. "How? I thought we were careful."

"Probably no one else even noticed, though you didn't really hide it well. Still, I make a habit of noticing what others do not. My life is circumscribed by arthritis so I must wring every drop from the life I contact."

Daniel shook his head in awe then sat silent for a time. "It would be bad enough if I just loved Kit, but I find that I still truly love Amanda too. It's tearing me apart. It's impossible."

"Well, very difficult at least. Love is to be shared. The trouble is that culture has declared that such loving is bad."

Once more Daniel was stunned by this old woman. "But I thought..."

"That I would condemn? Perhaps that I would punish you somehow?" She gave her head a minute shake. "I never condemn. I have too much to be condemned about," she said. "I do worry about the pain such a situation as this can cause all concerned."

She paused for a time, thinking. "How true is this feeling you have for Kit? Will it burn out after a little while?"

"I don't think so. I mean, I don't really know, but I don't think so. It feels as though she is deep, deep in my heart. Like Amanda. The only difference I can feel is history. Amanda's and mine is long. Kit's and mine is short."

"This has happened before? With other women?"

Daniel opened his mouth and closed it again, shocked at the baldness of the question. "No," he said at last. "I've been a faithful husband. I mean, I'm no saint. I've had my lustful moments when, if the proposition had been offered I might have cheated, but they came and went with no breach of faith. In some of my down moments I've even regretted not going for some of the other women who have offered, but regrets aren't cheating, are they?"

"According to Our Lord they are, but he held a rather high standard," she said with a wry twist of her mouth.

"Yeah, he did at that. But I'm not him. I'm not even one of his minor saints. Besides, I feel like this whole thing is out of my hands and has been from the start."

"Is that a true feeling, or an excuse?"

Daniel ran his eyes over the old woman's face. The question was not condemnation, only the desire for knowledge.

"I don't know, Elizabeth. Maybe an excuse, but I've run down the list of what ifs a thousand times. What if we hadn't come to church that first day? What if Kit hadn't come into Campo Redemptor, a place so small and out of the way I didn't even know it existed until that day? What if she had not just been talking to her fiancée and he hadn't just hurt her? What if, what if, what if?"

"Yes. What if. But you can what if yourself into a straight

jacket."

"I'm not far from that now. What am I going to do?"

Elizabeth chose not to let that question be rhetorical. "If you mean what should I do, the answer is obvious. Break it off with Kit and go home to Amanda who you say you still love. That would simplify everyone's lives."

That was so blunt and so true it was like a blow. He took a deep breath. "I can't Elizabeth. I can't."

"Then the second best action would be to tell Amanda. The pain would be great, but it would be over quickly and everyone could begin to heal."

That made Daniel flinch and his face flushed. "Easy for you to say," he answered, a little more sharply than he had intended. "You're not the one who has to do it."

"Very true, but you asked for my opinion and I gave it."

"But I can't do either one of those things—at least not yet."

"Then you have answered your own question," Elizabeth said. "You are, by your own free will, going to do nothing. Keep council with yourself only and continue forward. Let God or destiny or whatever, do what it will and deal with consequences as they come."

Daniel looked at his watch. It was 11:25.

Daniel left the Doyle's house at 12:30. He was as confused as before and now worried that Elizabeth might tell everyone what they had talked about. He didn't think she would, but anything was possible. It occurred to him that he had probably talked to the wrong Doyle about his troubles. After all, priests got paid to listen to confessions, even Anglican priests. But Elizabeth had seemed to be the one to talk to, so he had. He thought through the conversation again but at last shoved it into the bottom drawer of his mind and walked with determination. He was going to see Kit, and nothing else in the world mattered more than that.

He walked the same route he had come by in reverse and at the Accadamia he turned down the alley that led to Campo Redemptor. As he stepped into the Campo huge feathery flakes of snow began to fall.

The bar was as crowded today as it had been empty on that first day. Giorgio had another man, probably his son, behind the bar with him. They were dancing and whirling in the bartender's ballet delivering drinks as fast as they could pour. They had no time for conversation.

Daniel wedged himself up to the bar, asked the younger bartender for a cognac and a coffee. Giorgio looked up from the drinks he was pouring. "Coffee for the hands, Cognac for the feet," he said.

"I'm surprised you remember," Daniel said smiling.

"So beautiful a lady as yours, how could I forget."

Now Daniel really smiled—for a second. There was a hole in his middle that only Kit could fill and Giorgio had just reminded him that she was not there. "I'm waiting for her now," he said.

"Ah Bene," Giorgio answered. He turned away with a quick "Mi 'scuse" and carried on with his work.

The young bartender set the cognac before Daniel and the coffee beside it. Daniel warmed the Cognac in his hand for a moment then tossed it down his throat in one gulp. It burned and made his eyes water.

His mind would not leave his conversation with Elizabeth in the bottom drawer. It kept coming back to worry him. Of course she was right. The right thing to do would be to tell Kit that this must end. He had thirty years of history with Amanda. He had two sons with her. And more importantly, he loved her still. *I don't think I can though*, he thought. *Didn't we try this once before? Didn't I almost give up sleeping and take up self torture?*

He glanced at his watch. It was after one. *Maybe she won't come,* he thought. *Maybe she didn't get the message and maybe she won't come.* The pain of that thought was so great Daniel almost cried out. Instead he called for another Cognac.

The snow was falling heavier. It didn't usually snow much in Venice, but now the huge flakes were beginning to pile up. The cobblestones were going to be slick and dangerous.

Once more Daniel warmed the cognac in his hands for a moment then slugged it down. There was a glow in his belly from the first cognac; the second increased it to a fire.

How could I consider ending this with you Kit? He thought. *It would kill me. I think it would.*

The doubt demon that was never far from Daniel's mind whispered, *It's almost one thirty. She's not coming. Besides you don't really want her. She tricked you into this whole mess. You were almost over her when she came to Aviano. The Bitch was playing you like a fish on a line.*

But Daniel knew he was lying to himself. He hadn't been nearly over Kit. If she had not showed up on the steps that day he would have caved in sooner or later and come back to Venice seeking her.

"Another Cognac," Daniel said, then regretted it. *What are you gonna do fool?. Stand here and get drunk on your ass. You really ought to be sober enough to recognize Kit when she comes— If she comes.*

Daniel took the cognac glass in his hands and turned to look out the window. His doubts and fears had piled up and up until he was on the verge of screaming. Another bar patron wedged his way in front of Daniel and elbowed him in the belly. It was an accident, but the doubts and worries suddenly ignited and Daniel wanted to smash the man's face. He turned, set the still unfinished cognac on the bar and was in the process of drawing back his fist to punch the man beside him when Kit called out, "Daniel."

Daniel turned and there she was. All his rage and worry and doubt evaporated beneath her glad smile. The world had almost righted itself. He went to her and put his arms around her; Kit put hers 'round him, and the world was right again. They did not notice the glances and smiles from the other bar patrons.

IX

Amanda hadn't come home for lunch since they had been at Edwards. In Italy it had been the norm until Kit's death. Daniel would prepare a big Italian lunch for them and, like proper Italians, they would sit and eat and talk and laugh. Sometimes they even skipped lunch all together and made love in their sunny bedroom at the foot of the Alps, but that had all stopped. After Kit had died that had stopped. Daniel couldn't concentrate long enough to finish a meal, much less prepare one, and the few times Amanda had tried to coax him into making love it had ended in failure and tears. Now, in the desert, Amanda thought Daniel had begun to heal, and she hoped that they could return to having lunch at home together. Just a small thing. A small normalcy. It was with that in mind that she returned home at a little past noon thinking she would throw something together quickly and they would eat and— Well, there was no *and* yet. If they could eat together like they used to then maybe there could be an *and,* but for right now a simple meal would be enough.

Daniel wasn't in the kitchen or the living room and the TV was turned off. That was good. It probably meant he was in the office working. He had been doing that more lately. It was a hopeful sign. She walked to the office door and there was Daniel sitting before the computer, but his hands were covering his face and his shoulders shook in quiet sobs. On the computer screen was a piece of a poem.

"I think I cannot live without my Kit—
Since she is gone there is a hollow in my soul
That all the worlds created cannot fill..."

"Danny?" Amanda called.

He looked up and quickly tried to wipe his eyes and nose.

113

"I'm sorry 'Manda. I'm sorry. I just had this thought and I— I'm sorry."

Amanda was so torn! She wanted to hate him. She wanted to hate Kit. She wanted to turn and walk out of that office and just keep going, but she didn't. When Daniel had completely broken after Kit's funeral, and had been put in the hospital she had thought to file for a divorce, but she couldn't. As much as she wanted to she couldn't because she loved him. She wanted this pain to be over, but she couldn't abandon the only man she had ever loved. Amanda wanted Danny back! She wanted him back!

She went to him and put her arms around him, pulled his head against her waist. "What was the thought Danny? Was it the poem?"

Daniel shook his head against her. He took a deep breath and said, "It's just that I once told Kit that poetry is what poets do when their hearts are broken." He began to cry against her again and she stroked his hair. God how she loved him! God how she wanted him not to hurt anymore!

What do poets' wives do when their hearts are broken, she thought?

***

Amanda could see a change in Daniel after he came back from seeing Elizabeth. He told her all about the crowds and the train and the almost getting into a fight in a bar, but there was something else—a sea change. Several times in the next week she caught Daniel staring at her as though he had something to say, but was not quite sure how to say it. She willfully ignored the changes, chalking them up as one of Daniel's moods. *He has been moody and changeable ever since I have known him and this is no different,* but she knew it was.

The evening of Ash Wednesday Amanda and Daniel went to Venice. Canon Doyle had set himself to impose ashes three times during the day, morning, noon, and night. To save time the Pentland's drove rather than rode the train.

114

Venice was much changed between Fat Tuesday and Ash Wednesday. Everywhere the tattered remnants of MardiGras celebrations lay in the streets (trampled crepe paper streamers, confetti, popped balloons, scattered candies, broken porcelain) but the streets were almost empty of people.

St. George's was almost as empty as the streets. It was only Amanda, Daniel and another couple, but Canon Doyle continued as though the church were full. They knelt, prayed and went through the short service, then knelt at the altar rail for Canon Doyle to smudge the sign of the cross on their foreheads with ashes. It was a silent, solemn time, with no conversation before and little after.

On the way home Amanda said, "I'm going TDY again."

Daniel's heart jumped in his chest. Joy bubbled up but after a moment anxiety for Amanda damped the joy down. "Not back to Sarajevo," he said flatly.

"No. That was a fluke, and I promised I wouldn't volunteer any more, remember?"

He glanced from the road to her dim profile in the fading evening. A second later she turned to look into his eyes where he saw the truth of her promise. "OK, then where to?"

"Germany. Ramstein for a manning assist."

"Can't one of the other guys go?" Daniel asked. "Why you?"

"They need a Master Sergeant. Remember Lagasse from Rhein-Main?"

He thought about it for a moment. The Air Force was really a small town that happened to be spread all over the planet. It came to him at last. "Big guy? Fat? I thought he was gonna get put out for not making weight."

"They should have, but they didn't. Instead they put him in charge of Ramstein Logistics where he had a heart attack. I'm going to fill his slot until they can get a new guy in.

"How long will you be gone?"

"I don't know really. They are talking ninety days, but it

depends on how fast Randolph gets off its dead ass and gets somebody to fill the slot."

"So how come you wind up being the Kelly Girl? Didn't Preston tell them he needs you to change his diapers?"

"I'll be working for a General in Ramstein," she said with some pride. "Colonel Preston's diapers will just have to wait."

Daniel laughed. "True enough," he said.

Thoughts of Kit ran through his mind when he asked, "When do you go?"

"Friday."

"As in day after tomorrow?"

"Yeah."

"That's a lot of notice," he said cynically. It was only half an act. He thought he should seem upset with the short notice and he was, but he also about to burst with joyous laughing.

"Better than when we were in Germany. Remember? You were lucky to get a phone call."

"Yeah. Right. Doesn't make me like it any better though."

"What are you gonna do all alone in Italy?" Amanda asked.

Daniel glanced away from the road and toward Amanda. "Gimme a break, 'Manda I'll find plenty to do." He looked back at the road. "If nothing else I'll work nonstop on the book—or maybe I'll go to Rome. Would you hate me if I went to Rome?"

"Didn't we have this conversation once before?"

"Maybe. Did I go to Rome?" he asked, teasing.

"I don't think so."

"Um. I'm pretty sure I would have remembered it."

"Seriously Danny, you could go home to see your Mom or to Spain or even up to Germany.

"To stay with you?" He asked, with an eagerness that was a surprise to him— not sure why he had asked, or if he wanted her to say yes or no.

" No. I'll be too busy Danny! You know how this goes.

116

It's going to be twelve hours a day at least," she said.

He glanced again at her profile and suddenly knew that he was jealous; jealous of the Air Force for taking so much of her; jealous of her for being off to yet another adventure while he was stuck at home; jealous that somehow her life had *worked out* like she wanted and somehow his had not. The absurdity of it almost made him laugh at his own irrationality. He was a self centered child, crying for candy when mother had said not before dinner. A self centered child—

A switch in Daniel's mind clicked closed, shutting off his thoughts. "OK," he said.

"With this new dependant standby travel," Amanda continued, "You could hop anywhere in the world you wanted to."

"I'd need a bunch of paper work wouldn't I?"

"No. Just your ID card and a copy of the orders that brought us to Italy."

"Well, maybe I'll do that."

"Just see that you're back here in time to fix me a welcome home dinner," she said with mock severity.

"Yes mam. Just let me know when you're coming."

"So you can get rid of the floozies?"

Daniel's stomach did a roller coaster drop, but he managed a smile and said, "Yeah so I can get rid of the floozies."

Daniel dropped Amanda at the air terminal Friday morning. "If I don't answer the phone," he said, "It is because I decided to try hopping. Just leave a message on the machine. I'll call it every couple of days to pick up the messages, if I'm not stuck somewhere in the back of beyond because a flight got diverted to a place with no telephones."

"OK. I'll call you in a couple of days to let you know if this is really going take ninety days." She stretched up a little to kiss him goodbye. "I love you Danny," she said.

Daniel returned the kiss and pulled her to him in a bear hug. "I love you too 'Manda. Be safe, OK?"

"Head down and ass covered, Sir."

He let her go and she turned away. Daniel found that a part of him hated to see her go, even as another part of him was singing with gladness, and the same absurdity he had felt in the car sent a ghost to his mind. *It isn't natural to feel this way!* he thought. *I really may end up in that straight jacket Elizabeth was talking about.*

Daniel didn't even think about the train. He left the air terminal and headed toward the Venice Highway. He was leaning on Kit's gate post when she came home from class.

The next weeks were a gift from heaven.

Amanda called and said the headquarters squadron looked as though they had gone through a bombing. Everything in the office was misfiled or otherwise lost. "It may be the luckiest thing in the Air Force that Lagasse had his heart attack," she said. "Maybe I can unscramble this place enough so that if we go to war we can find the bullets."

Daniel laughed. "Finding the bullets won't help. We'd still need guns to shoot them out of."

"I'll be lucky to get out of here in 90 days Danny," she said. "If my replacement came in tomorrow I'd need a month to train him in place."

"Figures," Daniel said, trying to put all the cynical resignation into his voice that he thought he should be feeling.

"Are you doing all right?"

"Yeah. Not bad. I'm working some."

"That's good. Do you miss me?"

"You know I do. Be safe huh?"

"Safe? I'm in mortal danger of being sliced to death by paper cuts, but I'll watch myself."

Daniel laughed. "Just see that you do. I don't want you back here looking like hamburger."

Sometimes in Dreams

***

Daniel and Kit spent as near to every moment together as they could manage. During the week, when Kit was in school, Daniel stayed in Venice. He would walk around the city, visit the museums, read, even work on his book, but he would be waiting in Bar Redemptor at 1:00 PM every day, and every day his heart would soar at his first glimpse of her.

Kit's smile was always wide and warm when she first caught sight of him. They knew that they completed each other. They held pieces of one another inside themselves so deep and so hard that the pieces became parts of themselves, not of one another.

At night they slept in Kit's narrow bed and neither minded the constant touch of the other's body. Lying spoon fashion one night, after they had made quiet delicious love Daniel said, "We are really only one person you know. One spirit in two bodies." He stroked his hand down her side from shoulder to knee and back, then reached over and gently cupped her silken breast. "I have lived fifty years and traveled thousands of miles looking for you and I didn't even know it until I found you. I love you Kit. I love you."

Kit took his hand from her breast and kissed the palm then hugged it to her again. "I can't understand how I ever lived without you," she said.

At the weekends they went to Marsure. On days when it was not raining or cold they hiked and bicycled all over the Friulian countryside. Kit brought sketch pads and water colors and sketched medieval village churches and fountains. She also made marvelous water colors of the countryside. Daniel was fascinated with watching her throw a half dozen lines onto paper then bring the lines to life with a few daubs of color.

When it rained they stayed in. Daniel at first tried to work a little each day, but it was impossible. After a little while Kit would come to the office door and stand, watching him, and his concentration would evaporate. He hungered for her so much that just knowing she was in the house made his mind wander to her.

One rainy Saturday afternoon Daniel was making another futile attempt at working when Kit asked, "Can I read some of your work?"

"You have. My lousy poetry."

"It was not lousy, it was wonderful, but I want to read some of your other work. The prose."

Daniel shrugged. "If you can stand it I can," he said. "Top drawer of the left hand file cabinet. You'll find a manuscript tied with a green ribbon there. It's called *Serpents and Doves.*"

Kit opened the drawer and pulled out the thick sheaf of paper. The green ribbon was faded to chartreuse and the paper was yellowed.

"You hold in your hands," Daniel said with a bitter twist in his voice, "My first Magnum Opus. An unprepossessing little story of a young man's involvement with a Baptist girl and the Baptist Guru who used her to get at the young man for his own perverse pleasures, all set against a background of the racial upheavals of the south in the mid-sixties. And in reading it you are in the company of Legion, because that is how many editors have handled that and said, 'Who the hell does this guy think he is anyway.'"

Kit could taste the bitterness of all the rejections in the room. "They hurt you terribly didn't they?"

Daniel shrugged. "If ya can't stand the heat stay out of the kitchen, as Harry Truman once said."

"Is it about you?"

"Not exactly. Some of the people and places are from my past, but the main characters are fictions and so is the situation— mostly."

Kit nodded and went to get her reading glasses. She came back to the office and sat in the rocking chair beside the window and began to read.

Daniel turned to watch her read and rock for a little while, but soon decided it was a waste of time and turned back to his computer. For the next four hours he managed to get many words in a line, and at the end of that, when he was brain fried and limp with fatigue, he turned to her again. There was a stack of pages in a pile on the floor and the chair was steadily rocking back and forth.

"Are you hungry?" he asked.

Kit looked up with her eyes still focused elsewhere, "Beg pardon?" She asked.

"Are you hungry? Shall I fix us something to eat?"

"Oh. Yes, I suppose I am."

"Good. I'll throw some Carbonara together. It'll just take a little while."

"Wonderful," she said, but Daniel wasn't sure if she had heard a word he said. She was already back reading the manuscript.

A half hour later Daniel called her to come and eat. There was no answer. He walked back to the office and found her still sitting in the rocker trying to turn the manuscript more toward the window to catch the fading light.

Daniel flipped on the over head light and said, "Great invention. Let's you read after dark. Come and eat."

Kit's eyes focused on Daniel and the look stabbed his heart. Tears stood in her eyes. "Oh Daniel, those poor people caught up in the riot. How could police officers be so cruel?"

Daniel caught up a breath and stared at her for a second, then said, "It was a different time and a different place." His voice was a little chokey, but he shook it off. "Come and eat. Leave that alone... Come and eat."

Kit shook her head. "I'll come and eat, but I won't leave this alone. It is wonderful and terrible Daniel, and I don't know why someone hasn't published it. I want to finish it."

Daniel looked long at her lovely face and her tear shiny eyes and wondered if her judgment was clouded by love or if the book was really as good as she thought. He thought it was and Amanda had thought it was, but no one else seemed to have thought so. He put the thought aside and they ate Carbonara that was starting to go cold. Afterward, while Daniel washed the dishes and straightened the kitchen Kit went back to reading.

Later, in bed, Kit asked, "Did you really love her as much as that Daniel?"

Daniel rolled the question around in his mind for a while before answering. "I thought I did at the time. It took a while to get over her. I've been told that I give my heart away too easily and so get it broken a lot."

Kit brushed her lips against his and put an arm and a leg over him protectively. "I won't ever break your heart Daniel. I promise I won't."

Daniel pulled her closer to him as if to weld them into one creature. *I hope that's true, Kit* he thought. *Dear God I hope that's true.*

The Saturday morning after Easter the telephone in Marsure rang and Daniel picked up. "Pronto." he said.

"Hello?" Said a voice that was English and female. "I'm looking for Kit Marlowe, is she there with you?"

"Yes, hold on a second." He covered the receiver with his hand and called, "Kit it's for you. Marcy I think."

Kit came out of the bedroom frowning. "I told them not to call me here unless it was important," she said.

Daniel handed her the phone and stepped back.

"Hello Marcy, is that you?"

Marcy talked for a time with no need for anything from Kit. Kit suddenly grew pale and said "Oh God. When?"

A few minutes of listening passed. Daniel watched her, but there was nothing to hear. After a moment Kit seemed to shrink and blank shock filmed her sapphire eyes as she looked up into his face. She looked as though she wanted to cry but couldn't. "Throw my things in my grip please Marcy," she said at last. "I'll be there as soon as I can. And thank you. Thank you so much." She hung up the phone and turned to Daniel, eyes wide with shocked disbelief. "My Da had a heart attack," she said. "He died."

Daniel crossed himself then took her in his arms. "I'm so sorry, Kit. Christ I'm sorry. Let's get you on a plane."

She nodded woodenly and went to pack the few things she had brought with her while Daniel got on the telephone to Marco Polo Airport. There were no flights from there until the following day, but Al Italia said they had a flight going from Milan at five that afternoon. "We'll take it," Daniel said. "For one." He raised his voice. "Kit, round trip or one way?"

There was silence for a time before she said, "One way. I don't know when I can get back. My mother will be a wreck."

"One way," Daniel said with a foreboding in his stomach all out of proportion to the facts.

"Very well signor. Check in is two hours before departure. You may pick up the ticket at the Al Italia counter at Milano."

"Thank you," he said and hung up.

Kit came out with her black backpack hanging on one shoulder and her sketch pad under her arm. She still had shed no tears, but her eyes held that wide dry look of one holding on by their fingernails. "When I talked to him just last week he was hale and hearty," she said. "He should have lived a hundred years."

Daniel gave her a quick supportive hug and kissed her forehead, thinking, *it's just another cruel joke from the gods.*

X

It was July and hot. The desert sun at noon could blister skin in five minutes, but at night the temperature dropped into the seventies.

Daniel had taken to sitting on the patio at night looking toward the desert hills. He hardly slept through the night but when he did the dreams seemed to have eased. Amanda had thought he was getting better for a time, but that all seemed changed now. He did not seem to care about anything. He didn't cook at all anymore, or eat, or go to the gym, or do anything except sit in front of the TV. It almost didn't matter if it was on or not. He simply sat. He no longer went into the office for anything. He used to sit at his desk to write checks for the bills, but Amanda discovered he was no longer doing that through coming home one day to a stack of Over Due notices.

Amanda did something she had never before done. She sneaked into the office and looked at what Daniel had been working on in the lull when she thought he was healing. Before she had always waited until Daniel thought a piece was ready before she read it. She had looked forward to those times. They were as intimate as making love. More so in some ways. Making love she only touched his body. In reading his work she touched his soul.

What she found were fragments of poems about Kit, and a couple of paragraphs about the sound of the desert wind and how it was speaking to him. None of it gave any more insight into Daniel's mind than simply looking at him had. At last Amanda reached her wits end and she said, "Danny, you need to go see somebody again. You are beginning to really scare me. It's almost like right after—"

Daniel cut her off with, "I'm all right 'Manda. I'll be all right."

"Danny, it has been two years since Kit died!"

Daniel looked at Amanda as though she had slapped him, but she continued. "It's time for you to start living again. If you need to go back to the hospital that's OK. I love you and I don't want you to hurt anymore. You stopped taking your medicine."

He started to deny it but she snapped, "I've seen you flush them down the toilet! Please! I'll make an appointment for you with Dr. Sherman at Mental Health. He can help you not to hurt anymore"

Daniel laughed bitterly. "He's done me so much good so far," he said.

"Danny, you've got to want to get better. They can help you if you want to get better. They can help you sleep."

Daniel ran his eyes over his wife's face. She was still lovely in his eyes, and he still loved her, but he had hurt her so much. So much. But she still loved him in spite of it all and she was determined to help him live no matter what. It was in her eyes. He lifted his hand and touched her cheek. "OK," he said. "Make the appointment and I'll go."

Amanda nodded, satisfied. She left him sitting on the patio and went to bed.

***

The drive back from Milan was a horror. A spring storm that had rain, snow, and sleet followed him from the airport. The weather was so terrible that it didn't allow Daniel any leisure to be moody. He was too busy staying alive on the road. He had put Kit on the airplane and wished with all his heart that he could have gone with her. She looked so fragile and bereft! Eyes shock wide and dry, with the thinnest of gauze curtains pulled between them and the world.

Daniel kissed her and held her in the last moments before she went through the gate to the plane, but it was as though she wasn't really there. "Kit, I love you," he said. "If you need me just let me know. I'll be on the next thing smoking for England."

"I'll be back as soon as I can Daniel." She kissed him. "Thank you for loving me." She pulled herself out of his arms and went down the ramp.

When he made it back to Marsure he was exhausted, but he couldn't sleep. Alone in the house he rattled around like the last bean in a can, going from kitchen to living room to office to bedroom. About 2 AM he realized what he was doing. He was looking for Kit. His mind knew she was in England by now, but the little child in his spirit could not accept that. He finally lay down on the bed determined to force himself to sleep. He pulled the other pillow over his face and noticed that it smelled vaguely like Kit's hair, and then he remembered nothing until the next morning.

The next week was like the days after Kit had decided that they should not see each other anymore. Daniel ran and worked out until his body was drained, but the only way he could sleep was to pull the pillow that smelled like Kit's hair over his face. *What the hell am I gonna do when that smell fades?* he thought.

At 8:00 AM Saturday morning, four days after Kit had gone, the phone rang. Daniel was on it like a shot. No civilized "Pronto" or "Hello," no thought that it might be Amanda. He snatched the receiver off the cradle and said "Kit?"

"How did you know?" She asked.

"Simple. It was going to be you or I was going to slide over into crazy land. How are you? I miss you. I love you."

Kit laughed with delight. "I miss you terribly Daniel. Just hearing your voice helps me breathe easier."

"So, how are things going there?"

"The funeral was yesterday. It was nice. The church was full."

"How's your Mom holding up."

"About like I expected. We have cried rivers together, but she seems better today. I think having the funeral over has helped."

"And you. How are you?"

There was just a little more pause than the question justified and then she said, "I'm all right."

"Maybe so, but you're a lousy liar. Tell me the truth."

"No I really am all right—about Da and the funeral. I'm sad, but I'm fine."

"But there is something else."

"Daniel you have not known me long enough to be able to read my mind."

"I can read my own, and I meant it when I said we are one person. Now tell me what's wrong."

The sound of Kit taking a deep breath came down the phone line, and then she said, "David came to the funeral. He wants me to come back to him. He wants us to get married as soon as possible."

"I hope you told him to shove it up his ass."

A nervous little laugh answered the crudity. "Not precisely that way, but yes. I told him it was impossible and that I had met someone who loved me. He was furious. We had a terrible row Daniel."

"I thought I hated that guy the first time I heard his name, now I'm sure. What kind of an asshole broaches that kind of subject at a funeral? That takes a truly insensitive lout."

The nervous laugh again. "That's David. I never knew what a miserable excuse for a human being he was until I met you."

Daniel laughed at the way that came out. "No need for flattery sweet, I'm so deep in love with you you'll never get rid of me."

"I am so glad... Daniel?"

"I'm here."

"Daniel," she hesitated again then went ahead with a

rush. "Daniel, I need you with me. I hurt so bad when you are away from me, and now with Da and David and all—"

"I'm on my way there," he said without a second's hesitation. "I think there's a military hop to Mildenhall this afternoon or tomorrow. But one way or another I'll be with you tomorrow. Can you hang on that long? There is the Al Italia flight out of Milan this afternoon."

"I can wait until tomorrow," she said relief clear in her voice.

"Give me a number where I can reach you," he said, and wrote down the string of numbers she reeled off. "I'll call you as soon as I land in England."

"I can hardly wait. I love you so much Daniel."

"See you soon."

Daniel called the Military terminal the second he hung up with Kit. There was indeed a hop that went at 1400 (2:00 PM). It was a C-130 which made him grimace. C-130's were cargo planes, not really meant to carry people, but any bird was better than no bird.

He dug out copies of PCS (Permanent Change of Station) orders, his passport and the $300 in cash he had hidden in his desk then threw some clothes and toiletries into his backpack, stuck his tweed hat on and headed out the door before he remembered Amanda.

He turned back into the foyer to the phone answering machine. He held the "record a message" button down and said. "Amanda, I have gone to England. I'll call here when I get there and tell you where you can reach me. Bye."

He listened to the message again and, satisfied, headed for the air terminal. He parked the car in Amanda's slot at work and walked the last half mile down to the terminal.

Aviano Air Terminal was barely controlled chaos most of the time. What used to be a quiet little TDY base at the foot of the Dolomite Alps had turned into the transit hub for every man, machine, or morsel that was on its way to Bosnia-

Herzegovina or the MiddleEast. It was bursting at the seams and today 'zoo' seemed far too mild a description. The cramped waiting room of the terminal was jammed with people waiting for the weekly contract Freedom Bird that left for Philadelphia. Families moving with every chick and child were sitting atop their suitcases waiting for the boarding call. Mothers and fathers, already haggard from days of clearing paperwork and cleaning quarters, were doing their best to keep children, excited to bursting, corralled long enough to get them bedded down on the plane for the eight hour flight across the Atlantic.

Daniel pushed through the crowd and presented his orders and ID card at the desk. Aviano, despite its crowded condition, was still a small military community so it was no surprise that he knew the male Senior Airman behind the desk. "How're chances of getting on the Mildenhall hop, Jimmy?" Daniel asked.

The senior airman, looking crisp and business like in razor creased blues, glanced up from a stack of papers and grinned. "Not so bad Mr. Pentland. I'll be able to tell you better when we get this mob on the Freedom Bird. Take this—"he handed Daniel a slip of paper, "Fill it out and time stamp it right there—"he indicated the square on the paper and the time clock to the left of the desk. "Then write your name, your classification—you're Class 3 unaccompanied dependant—and the time from the stamp in the book marked Mildenhall. You got all your other paperwork?"

"Orders, passport, and ID card. That's all I need right?"

"Right. Then have a seat—if you can find one. We'll call the flight at about 1315, if the plane doesn't break. Standby gets called fifteen minutes before wheels up."

Daniel said thanks and went to do as he was told. The time was 0930.

There were no seats. Daniel and perhaps twenty other people moved in a kind of circular pattern around the edges of the occupied orange chairs like vultures looking for road kill. If a seat came open for a second someone's behind filled it the next second.

At 1100 the first boarding call for the Freedom Bird came and with a great groan and inrush of breath the waiting area began to clear.

Daniel parked himself practically under the desk when an orange chair came open. He spotted any number of people he knew, but didn't want to talk to anyone so he kicked back in the chair and pulled his hat down over his eyes. It didn't help. Colonel Preston, Amanda's boss happened to be in the waiting room and he came over to Daniel. "Hey Dan," he said.

Daniel gritted his teeth and pushed his hat back. He didn't like Preston at the best of times which this wasn't. "Colonel." he said.

"Where you off to?" Preston asked, sitting down beside him.

Daniel cursed the fate that left the chair beside him empty, but saw that he was not going to shake loose of Preston easily, so he put on his hale-fellow-well-met, hardy traveler persona and said, "Thought I'd hop up and see the Queen for a couple of days. I hear the old girl's been feeling poorly."

"Oh to be in England now that Spring has come... or something like that."

"Yeah. I hear the rain drops are only quart size in the spring."

The colonel laughed. "It shouldn't have been a surprise to anyone that the Brits built an Empire in tropical places. Their weather is so rotten they'll do anything to get away from it."

"Say, as long as I have you here, would you happen to know when Amanda is coming back? She called way back at the beginning of this and said the place was such a mess she might get a short tour ribbon out of it, but I think she was kidding— wasn't she?"

Preston shrugged. "Actually you seem to know more

about it than I do. Last I heard they were going to need her right through the ORI (Operational Readiness Inspection) in June."

"June? Christ on a crutch! She will get a short tour ribbon!"

"We sure miss her down here. The office has been barely functional since she left," Preston said. It gave Daniel a moment of pleasure to see this arrogant airplane driver hung out on his own.

Preston leaned back as though he would stay all day, but he didn't say anything else for quite a while. Daniel was almost ready to try kicking back under his hat again when the Colonel said, "Hey, that was some beautiful red head I saw you with the other day."

Daniel's heart snagged between beats. "When was that, Sir?" he asked, hoping he didn't sound as bad to Preston as he did to himself.

"I don't know, couple of weeks ago I guess. Up toward Barcis. You were on bicycles."

"Oh, that was Kit," Daniel said trying to sound off hand. "She's a British exchange student studying architecture at the University in Venice. We met her at church down there. St. George's."

The colonel nodded. "Sure was beautiful. I wouldn't have minded riding a few miles behind her."

Daniel's temper went up two degrees. If Preston had been noticing he would have seen Daniel's jaw muscles twitch. But Daniel maintained his cool. *All I need is to blow my top and punch this dumb sonofabitch out,* Daniel thought. *I'd be in custody in a heartbeat.* He jammed his hands beneath his arm pits as though he was chilly, but it was to keep them from balling into fists.

"She is beautiful, no doubt about it," Daniel said.

"Amanda know about her?"

Superior officer or not, Daniel wasn't going to take much more. "Kit is a friend of ours, Sir." There were icicles hanging off the "Sir."

Preston lifted his hands. "No offense. Pure admiration."

"Of course—Sir."

Preston finally got it through his thick skull that his presence was no longer welcome and got up. "Hope you get your flight. Enjoy England."

"Thank you, sir."

Preston grinned, turned on his heel and went.

Daniel took his hands from beneath his arms and found that they were shaking with unspent rage.

"This is first call for flight 122 to Mildenhall, England. All ticketed passengers holding PCS or TDY orders please report to gate 5."

Daniel's heart rate went up with the announcement. He looked at his watch. 1315 just as Jimmy had said. A few uniformed people stood at the call and moved toward gate five. He was glad to see it was so few.

Second call came ten minutes later. "All persons holding valid leave orders please report to gate 5." A young couple got up and headed for the gate.

At 1340 the announcement came. "All class three and four passengers holding time stamped form 1138 for Mildenhall, England, please report to gate 5."

Daniel slung his pack over his shoulder and went. A half dozen others also rose and went toward the gate. Jimmy, the airman from the desk, was now inspecting paperwork at the gate. He grinned when he saw Daniel. "I'd say chances are pretty good Mr. Pentland. May I see your paperwork please?"

Jimmy took the papers, looked them over, stamped the form 1138 and gave them back. Then he reached into a box beneath the desk and came out with a box lunch in a pink box. "Baloney and cheese," he said grinning. "Sticks to the ribs or to the floor if the flight gets rough. Ear plugs are in the box."

Daniel took the box, returned the grin and shook his head.

"You're a cruel man, Jimmy."

"It's one of the few joys of my life, sir. Please remove your hat and hang on to it tight when you walk across the apron to the plane. Wouldn't want to FOD (Foreign Object Damage) an engine out now would we?"

The flight took four hours. C-130's might be the most reliable airplane ever built, but they were slow and noisy and cold. By the time they landed in England Daniel was almost deaf from the engine roar, ear plugs not withstanding, and so stiff with cold he needed help to get out of his sling seat. He felt like an old man until he saw several younger men in need of the same assistance. He felt as though he had been beaten with a fire place poker, but he was in England. It was 6:00PM.

Customs was easy. They asked the usual questions (business or pleasure, how long will you stay) then stamped his passport and let him through into the waiting area. He saw a bank of phones and went to them only to discover that he didn't have any English coins. There was a gift shop in the terminal but it was closed and the change bank was closed too. He happened to glance outside and see a yellow and black checkered Taxi sitting in front of the terminal, the driver leaning against it with a smoke dangling from his lip. Daniel went to him.

"Taxi, Sir?" the driver said perking up. His accent seemed thicker than Kit's somehow. Certainly different.

"Maybe. Is there any place around to get some money changed?"

"Sure. NCO Club here on base. I'll take you."

"I don't have any Pounds."

"That's all right, guv. I trust ya." He opened the back door for Daniel.

Daniel left the Taxi sitting outside the NCO Club with the meter running, went in and changed all his American dollars to

Pounds then went to the phone and dialed the number Kit had given him. The phone didn't even finish one ring before it was picked up. "Daniel?" Kit said.

Daniel laughed with delight. "I told you we were one person," he said.

"Where are you?"

"East Anglia, at Mildenhall."

"You're still a long way from here."

"New Castle, right?"

"Yes."

"There is bound to be a train or a bus or something around here. I'll find it and be on it as soon as I can."

"No, Daniel. No." Kit sounded odd. Apprehensive.

"What's wrong, love?"

"Nothing."

"We went through this before. You can't lie to me. What's wrong?"

Static crackled down the wire for a moment. "It's David. He keeps hanging about and demanding that I talk to him."

Daniel's stomach and voice tightened. "That can be fixed," he said. "I'll have a word with him when I get there."

"No Daniel. Please. Let me come to you."

"But your Mom."

"Mum is fine. My brother Alfred is here to stay with her for a couple of weeks. I can come there easily."

Daniel hesitated. He really wanted to go to New Castle and teach this David some manners, but Kit seemed pretty set against that. "I don't know anything about this area," he said. "I don't even know if there is a hotel around here we could stay in."

"Then let's meet in London."

"That's a long way from you isn't it?"

"That is partly the point. It is a long way from here."

Daniel licked at the corner of his mouth and thought about it. "OK," he said at last. "Where shall we meet?"

Kit was silent for a time, obviously thinking. "You go to Paddington station" she said. "Near there, in a place called Sussex Gardens, there are simply hundreds of Bed and Breakfast Inns. Go there, get a room and call me again. If I'm not here Mum or Alfred will give you the information."

"Sounds complicated. Can't I just come there?"

"No, Daniel. Please," she begged. "Do this for me. Because you love me."

That stabbed him. "That is a dirty trick to ask like that."

"I'm sorry, but please do it my way," Her voice was firm now— expecting to get her way.

"OK. OK. We'll do it your way," he said with a resigned sigh.

"Wonderful. I'll have news for you when you call me back."

"All right. Sussex Garden near Paddington Station. I'm on my way. I love you."

"I can't wait until I see you. I miss you so much it hurts."

"I love you," Daniel said again, but she was already gone.

Outside the taxi driver was leaning against his cab smoking another cigarette "Hello guv," he said. "All fixed then?"

"Yeah. How do I get to London?"

"Well, motor bus is the cheapest. I think there is one from the base tomorrow morning—no wait, tomorrow is Sunday."

"Could you take me?"

The driver got a calculating look on his face then dismissed the thought with a shake of his head. "Cost you a bloody fortune," he said and shrugged. "I don't mind the odd extra mile to pad the meter, but that would be thievery outright. I think your best idea is British Rail from Ely."

It was 10:00 PM and rain was falling steadily as the train pulled into Kings Cross Station. Daniel remembered then that his umbrella was standing in the hall closet in Marsure. Not that it had mattered yet. When he got off the train he was under the station roof and he went directly to the information booth in the center of the station. He picked up a map there and with only a couple of mistakes made his way down to the Underground. He rode it round to Paddington Station and got off. Since he had stepped foot on the Ely station platform he had not been out from under a roof until he left Paddington.

According to the map Sussex Garden was only a couple of blocks from the station, but in the pouring rain it felt more like a couple of miles. He was dressed for the weather, but was still dripping when he reached the place. Kit had been right. As far as he could see in either direction, on both sides of the divided street there were small lighted signs saying Bed and Breakfast.

Daniel turned into the first place on the left. The lobby was painted like a Greek temple with pillars and god statues. It gave him a chill for some reason. The man behind the desk was olive skinned, with black curly hair and a white smile. He was dressed in the wide sleeved white shirt and red embroidered vest every movie Greek had worn since silent films. "Good evening," he said in a perfect London accent. "Miserable weather isn't it? Would you like a room?"

"Yes. For two," Daniel answered taking his hat off carefully so as not to drip on the carpet.

"Two?"

"Yes. My—" Daniel did not quite know what to call Kit. My lover, my paramour, my mistress? "My wife will be along either late tonight or tomorrow morning. By the way, can I make a long distance phone call from my room?"

"Yes of course. It will be charged to your bill. May I see your passport please? "

Daniel handed it over and the clerk made a copy of it then handed it back.

In a few moments all the formalities were finished and Daniel was given his key. The room was three flights up and there was no elevator, but that didn't matter. Daniel was glad to simply be near the end of a grueling day. He trudged up to the room, dumped his back pack on the double bed and went to the phone. He picked it up and the clerk below connected him through an old fashioned switch board to an outside line. Daniel dialed the string of numbers again and was surprised when the phone in New Castle rang four times before someone picked up.

"Hello, are you there?" The voice of an older woman asked.

"May I speak with Kit Marlowe?"

"She isn't here. Is this Daniel?"

"Yes Mam."

"You needn't Mam me," the woman said with a chill in her voice. "I understand that we are contemporaries."

Daniel was taken aback by the hostility. "Yes, I suppose we are," he said. There was a silence so piercing it ran down the phone line and drove itself into Daniel's temple.

"I hope you don't think that this is just some mid-life crisis that your daughter is caught up in Mrs. Marlowe," Daniel said rather more pleadingly than he intended. "I promise you it isn't. I love her and she loves me." He stopped and listened for some reaction but none came.

"I don't know how this is going to come out," he went on, "but I would rather die than hurt her."

There was more silence from New Castle, but it was followed by a sniff which might have been from tears. "Kit said almost the same thing not an hour ago." her mother said. "I hope love will be enough."

Daniel sighed. "So do I Mrs. Marlowe. So do I. Did Kit leave a message for me?"

"Yes. Her train will arrive at Euston Station at Five O'clock tomorrow morning."

"Thank you. Please believe that I am sorry for the loss of your husband. I hated to take Kit away from you at a time like this, but she insisted she come here rather than have me come there. If you need us for any reason please call. You can reach us at…" Daniel looked at the pad lying beside the phone, and reeled off the telephone number. "That is the Hotel Cassandra in Sussex Garden." As he said the name the chill from the lobby ran up his spine again.

"Very well then," Mrs. Marlowe said, less hostile but still not content. "Good night Mr. Pentland."

"Good night," he said and hung up the phone. He glanced at his watch. It was midnight. Daniel had been going almost twenty four straight hours and he was exhausted. He took off his wet coat and hat, hung them in the bathroom and lay on the bed. He thought about setting the alarm clock that sat on the table beside the bed but then laughed. *Yeah, like I'm gonna sleep!*

XI

It was already hot in the house when the alarm clock woke Amanda. She turned it off and squeezed her eyes shut two or three times to get the last of the sleep sand out of them. Amanda had been dreaming, and she hated to leave the dream behind. In it the world was right again. She had been swimming in a pool of warm water that caressed her all over. Daniel, naked and smiling, had reached out to her and she had taken his hand. They were one again, together and happy. There was no Kit.

Amanda looked over at Daniel's side of the bed. It was empty, but that was no surprise. She hadn't heard him dreaming, but he had slept so little of late that she was used to his getting up in the middle of the night and going to the living room or patio.

She got up and went through the regular week day morning routine of quick shower, a little makeup, into a uniform and head out for work with a cup of coffee in her hand, but this morning's routine ended with walking into the kitchen. There was no coffee. She had forgotten to set up the pot and turn on the timer. "Damn!" she said. It used to be Daniel's job to do the coffee, she thought. *Where is he anyway?* She went back to the living room and across to the sliding glass patio door. He wasn't outside either.

"Danny? Where are you?" She called. There was no answer and the silence gave her a sick feeling. She went and checked both bathrooms then back to the bedrooms and finally the office. She found the note lying on the desk. It said—

"I am sorry I hurt you so much Amanda. It was my fault Kit died. If I had never loved her she would be alive. I am sorry about so much. Please tell Jack and Mitch their father

141

was a fool and they are better off without him, and so are you."

It was signed with his full name. Daniel R. Pentland.

"Oh my God, Oh my God," Amanda said. She threw down the note and made another frantic search of the house, expecting to find Daniel's body in every room, but she didn't. At last she went to the garage. It was the only place left. She steeled herself and opened the door. The car was gone.

***

It did not matter that getting to London had brought Daniel to the verge of collapse from exhaustion, he still couldn't sleep. He drifted in and out of a shallow unconsciousness, but only for a few moments at a time. He even tried putting the other pillow over his face, pretending it was the one from his own bed that smelled of Kit's hair, but it didn't work.

At 0230 he gave up, got up, showered, and dressed. His coat and hat were still dripping wet, but he put them on anyway.

The rain had stopped and there were stars. It was cold. The streets were empty. He walked to the Paddington Station Underground and waited twenty minutes for the train. Subways didn't run as often at 0300 and no wonder. He was the only passenger in Paddington Station and looked to be the only one on the train.

Euston Station was a little more lively. Daniel read the big board and found that the train from New Castle was on time and arriving on track 23, but not for another hour. He spotted a tea shoppe that was open and went there, picked up a cup of strong black tea and a scone and went to a bench beside Track 23. When the tea and scone were gone there was nothing left to do but to sit and endure, so that was what he did.

I must look like some derelict trying to get sober, he thought.

The rumble of a train brought him to his feet. It was 0455.

His back and legs ached with weariness, but that was all forgotten in the up rush of gladness the train sliding up beside him brought. At 0500 on the dot the train jerked and rattled to a complete stop and doors popped open. People began to trickle off the train.

Daniel, being over six feet tall, could look over most people's heads, but in order to be seen better he stepped up onto the bench he had been sitting on. In moments his anxiety began to show. He danced from foot to foot as though the bench were hot.

A woman in a long camel colored duffel coat with the hood up, obscuring her face stepped down from the train and looked up and down the platform. She had a black knapsack over her shoulder. It was Kit. She spotted Daniel standing on his bench and waved, and the world became right again.

Daniel stepped down and headed toward her. It was all he could do to keep from breaking into a run. She dropped her bag and melted into his arms. He covered her mouth with his own. His heart was singing and shouting and his mind echoed the simple prayer, *Thank you God! Thank you!*

Breathless between kisses Kit said, "I missed you so much. I love you. I live for you."

Daniel held her away from him so that he could look into her face and assure himself that she was real, but the warm love was suddenly replaced with shock. He lifted his hand and pushed the hood of her coat back to make sure he was really seeing what he thought. He was. Kit's left eye was black and blue and her cheek was swollen and bruised. "Who did this?" he said, all quiet rage. "No, never mind, I know who did it. David."

Kit put her face against Daniel's chest and held tight to him. "It's all right. I'm all right. It doesn't hurt now."

Daniel tightened his arms around her protectively. His rage was boiling. "If I ever lay eyes on that son of bitch I'll kill him," he said.

"That's why I didn't want you to come to New Castle. I was afraid David would hurt you or you him and I couldn't stand that. Not on top of everything else."

"Has this happened before?"

Kit was silent, still pressing her face against his chest.

"It has hasn't it? Answer me."

In a small voice she said, "Not for a long time. The last time was a couple of years ago. Da found out about it. He went after David with a masons hammer."

"I had a feeling I would have liked your father. He should have killed him."

"He threatened to."

"Why didn't you tell David to go to hell after that?"

"I did. I told him I was through with him. I even went to Australia, but when I came home he begged me to take him back. He promised it would never happen again. Mum and Da said I should tell him to go to blazes, but he was so pathetic— so I took him back. He never hit me again."

"Until your father was safely dead and couldn't protect you anymore." He felt Kit go stiff against him and it dawned on him how cold he had sounded. "I'm sorry. I didn't mean to be so hard about it."

"It's done now. I told David I would have the police on him if he ever came around again. He's finished."

They stood holding each other for a little while longer, then Daniel said, "Let's get out of here. I have a room in Sussex Garden. I want to make love to you. Soft and gentle to make you forget everything but me."

Kit squeezed him tight. "Oh yes, please. I thought about only that all the way here. I've thought of almost nothing else for days."

They made desperate hungry love filled with grasping, holding, touching; filled with tears and joy; filled with the delicious agony of release, then they slept still entangled in one another.

When they woke it was afternoon. They made love again. This time slow and sensual as a silk scarf drawn lightly across the body.

Afterward Kit lay atop Daniel, her head on his chest. Her hair glowed like a halo in the afternoon sun coming through the window. His hands slowly stroked and combed through it, and he inhaled the perfume of it.

"The smell of your hair on a pillow back in Italy was the only thing that kept me sane," he said. "I need you Kit. I want you and I need you. Without you—"

"Without me your life would be simple, so let's not talk about it," she interrupted.

Daniel brought a handful of her hair to his mouth and kissed it. "OK," he said. "We won't talk about it."

She moved a little and kissed his chest, then kissed his mouth and sat up still astride him.

"I wish you could make us omelets." she said.

Daniel smiled. "Oh, I see how it goes. Get one appetite taken care of and all she can think about is her stomach." He stroked his hands up her tummy and over her breasts.

Kit smiled. Her bruised face made it crooked, and Daniel again felt the acid in his stomach come to a slow boil. How could anyone ever lay hands on so beautiful a creature in any way but with loving gentleness? It was beyond his understanding.

"Well," he said after a moment. "I can't make us omelets, but I'm sure this fine city can supply us with something nearly as good."

"I am starving," she said and rolled off him. She went to the bathroom and in a moment Daniel heard the shower start. He wished the shower stall was big enough to allow them both inside at the same time. He would have loved to bathe her and shampoo her hair, but the stall was barely big enough for one so he lay quietly and listened to the water run.

After a few moments she came out all pink and glowing from the hot water and Daniel again had the coppery dry taste of awakened desire at the back of his throat. "You shouldn't do that," he said, teasing. "Dressed like that you won't ever get your omelet."

Kit grinned and held the towel in front of her with mock modesty. "Oh yes I will. I must. I'm too famished to be ravished. First food, then—" she flipped up the corner of the towel.

Daniel laughed and got up. "Sounds like a deal," he said and kissed her bare shoulder as he headed for the shower.

They settled for fish and chips. "But it is such a cliché, Daniel," Kit said, teasing. "You'd never let yourself get away with it in a story."

Daniel took another bite of the greasy deep fried cod and said around it, "things become clichés because they are so true. I want to do all the cliché things while we are here. I want to eat pub food..."

"Steak and Kidney Pudd..." She said.

"I want to go to the Tower of London..."

"Crown jewels and heads will roll..."

"...and Westminster Abby—"

"Poets corner?"

"Right. And hear Big Ben sound off..."

"It's just a big bell..."

"And hear a bobby say, *What's all this then*? Like the bobbies in all the Monty Python sketches."

"You Americans are all just tourists at heart, aren't you?"

"Absolutely. Photographs and trashy souvenirs are my life."

"I thought I was your life?" Kit said, still teasing, but she wanted the words back the next instant. All the teasing went out of Daniel.

"You are, Kit. I don't think I could live without you. I

certainly wouldn't want to live without you."

Kit shook her head, almost afraid of his passion; afraid that she felt the same way. "No one is worth that much Daniel. No one."

His gaze traveled over her face and came to rest locked with her eyes. "You are," he said.

She stroked his cheek, a half smile on her own face. "Will you say that when I'm a fat old biddy in a ratty wrapper and scuffs?"

A picture of Amanda, beautiful in her house coat with wet hair in a towel flickered through his mind, and he shoved it away. "Even when you are a fat old haus Frau," he said and kissed the tip of her nose.

Over the next three days Kit and Daniel walked all over London. During the day they did all the tourist things and then some, taking joy in simply walking hand in hand. At night they made love and slept in one another's arms. It was a perfect existence, a perfect world, a perfect dream; but like all dreams there had to come an awakening.

They stopped in the Rose and Crown pub near the Tate Gallery and ordered lunch. They were tired from walking and their eyes were full of sights so they rested and just looked at one another.

"Gawd, he's old enough to be your grandfather," a harsh male New Castle accent said in a loud voice.

The noisy pub quieted as if someone had thrown a switch.

A blast of adrenaline shot through Daniel and he turned to find a tall burly man, long haired, mustachioed and wearing an overcoat, standing behind him. The man's hands were jammed into the pockets of his coat and his mouth was twisted with disgust. His blue eyes smoldered with barely controlled anger. There was a distinct aroma of beer around him.

"What are you doing here, David?" Kit said.

"Come to tell this Yank bastard to sod off, and to take you

home."

Daniel rose from his chair, never taking his eyes off David's face.

"Here, Here, Gran-ther," David sneered. "Don't get yourself all upset. You'll bring on your rheumatism."

The publican who had been behind the bar stepped out with a barrel mallet in his hand. "Here now," he said. "I'll have no trouble in my bar."

"No trouble intended friend," Daniel said, lifting his hands shoulder high palms out. "Just minding our own business."

"David, I told you before that we were through. I told you I'd have the police on you if you ever came near me again. How did you find us?"

"I followed you. I been following you since yesterday."

"How? How did you find us?" Kit demanded.

"Your Mum."

"That's a lie," Kit said, strong and flat. "She wouldn't have told you anything unless—" She paled. "You didn't hurt her did you?"

David blinked and backed off a little. "Of course not! I don't hit—" he stopped and then said, "I read the hotel name off the telephone pad at your house when I went to ask where you were."

"So you're a liar as well as a woman beater," Daniel said, still not taking his eyes off David's face.

David's anger flared from drunken smolder to flame in an instant. He lunged at Daniel who took half a step to the right, stuck out his left leg and helped David to trip over it with a small push.

David went sprawling into the table and onto the floor at Kit's feet.

The publican lifted his hammer to waist height.

"As long as you're down there you son of bitch, maybe you ought to apologize to Kit for ever laying hands on her,"

Daniel said.

Kit pulled her knees around away from David. "I don't need an apology. I just want him gone."

"And I want yer all gone," the publican said. "Get out."

"But our food," Kit began.

"Forget it Kit, let's go," Daniel said.

Kit started to stand, but David wasn't finished. Still on his knees, he lunged at Kit and grabbed her wrist. She cried out with pain and that was all Daniel needed. The street-fighter came out without even a thought. He lifted his right foot and planted a vicious heel kick square on David's left kidney.

David screamed and tried to turn, but he did not let go of Kit's wrist. She cried out in pain again. Daniel stepped forward and clapped his cupped hands hard over David's ears, then opened his hands and did it again. David let go of Kit and grabbed the sides of his head. Blood was already running from his left ear.

Daniel grabbed a handful of David's hair and spun him around the rest of the way. David was still on his knees. The fight was gone out of him, but Daniel still had rage to spend. With the side of his half closed right fist he smashed down on the bridge of David's nose. Blood squirted from the nostrils. Daniel released his hair and David went down on his face.

It all happened so fast that the publican had no time to react. By the time he managed to shout "Stop it!" the fight was over. David was sprawled in a widening pool of his own blood and Daniel was kneeling at Kit's side asking, "Are you all right? Did he break your wrist?"

Forehead pale with pain and lips grey with on coming shock she said, "No, I'm all right Daniel. It hurts, but I don't think it's broken. What about David?"

"Fuck David. He should die."

Kit's eyes went wide as she looked at Daniel's face. "You really mean that don't you?"

Someone had called the Police and they chose that

moment to show up. Five blue suited, plug helmeted officers. Daniel stood to meet them and the one wearing sergeants stripes asked "What's all this then?"

Daniel heard it and began to laugh. It was unspent adrenaline reaction, and sounded hysterical. It stole the iron control of a moment before from Daniel's legs. He sat down in a chair still laughing. He was shaking as though he would never be warm again.

"You'd better see to that one," the publican said waving his hammer at David. "I think he's hurt bad."

One of the Bobbies squatted beside David and checked his pulse.

The laughter went out of Daniel. "Hell with him. See to Kit. I think that bastard broke her wrist. He's the one that blacked her eye."

"That true miss?"

"I don't know if it's broken, but it does hurt rather a lot."

The Bobby took in the yellowing bruises on Kit's face and filed them for later consideration.

"This one's alive," the other bobby said, "but he is pretty well stonkered."

"Call an ambulance," the sergeant said, and one of the officers did so.

David groaned and tried to lift himself.

"Easy there," said the Bobby. "Ambulance coming for you in a moment."

"Can we go officer?" Daniel asked. He was still shaking so hard he might not have been able to go if the Bobby had said he could.

"Not until this gets all sorted out sir. I'm afraid you'll have to come along with us."

Daniel clenched his teeth hard, about to protest, then thought better of it. "OK, fine. All right. But see to Kit's wrist. I'm pretty sure it's broken."

"We'll do that sir, I promise. Now come along—quietly if

you please."

"Yeah all right, all right," Daniel said, standing on wobbly legs. "Am I under arrest? Should I call my embassy?"

"No sir, you're not under arrest—yet. You can call the American Embassy from the station if you wish."

They did not put Daniel in handcuffs, but did walk out one on each side of him. There was a car waiting outside the pub with its blue gumball light spinning. They put him in the back seat. The last thing he saw through the car window as it pulled away was Kit, holding her wrist, standing in the door of the pub.

Four hours later Kit found Daniel sitting on a bench in the lobby area of the police station. Her left wrist had a cast on it.

"He did break it," Daniel said, disgusted. "Bastard! I should've killed him when I had the chance."

Kit put her arms around him as though calming an angry child. "You mustn't say that Daniel. He might die and if they hear you saying that."

"I doubt if he is going to die," Daniel said. "He should for that." he touched the cast, "and for that," he kissed her bruised eye. It was healing now. Turning from black and blue to yellow-green and red.

Kit looked deeply into his eyes. There was something fearful there and it made her shudder. "You're frightening me, Daniel. Don't say that any more. Please."

He took a deep breath and let it out slowly. "I'm sorry," he said, contritely. "I won't say it anymore.

She hugged him.

"Oh. Hello, miss," the sergeant who had been at the Rose and Crown said. He glanced at the cast on Kit's wrist. "So, it was broken, eh?"

"Yes sir."

"Well then, all the better."

Daniel frowned.

"Here, here," said the sergeant. "No need to look so

fierce, Mr. Pentland. I've good news. Everyone in the Rose and Crown agrees that the other fellow started the whole thing, and that you were just protecting the lady. That cast and that eye pretty well say that there was something to protect her from."

"How is David?" Kit asked.

"Kidney's bruised, but not ruptured. One ear drum burst, and his nose won't ever be the same. He'll live."

"No assault charges? Nothing like that?" Daniel asked.

"We asked if he wanted to serve charges, but he said no. In view of the circumstance we didn't push too hard."

Daniel gave a relieved sigh. "Does that mean we can go now?" he asked.

The sergeant passed a calculating look over Daniel, then over Kit, then back to Daniel.

"Mr. Pentland, I can't fault a man for protecting his woman, but you came close to killing that arse hole—begging your pardon miss—that fool today. If you had, you and this lovely lady would have been apart for a long, long time. Perhaps you had best consider that next time before you put your heel into a man's kidney."

Daniel looked into the sergeants eyes and didn't turn away. "Right Oh, sergeant," he said.

"It won't happen again," Kit promised for him. "I'll see to that."

The sergeant shifted his gaze to Kit. After a moment he said, "Very well then. You're free to go. I don't want to see either of you again."

Daniel stood and offered his hand to the sergeant who took it and squeezed just a little. Daniel winced. His hand was sore from the last shot he had given David. The sergeant grinned and said. "Glad to see you didn't come out completely unmarked. Wouldn't seem fair somehow."

Daniel answered with a sheepish grin. "I'll have nightmares about it for the next month," he said. "I hate fighting."

XII

There were several people in the house with Amanda now; mostly women from the base chapel. Amanda had called Major Quinn the head chaplain shortly after she had called the Security Police to report Daniel missing, and the Major had begun putting out the word that drew the chapel support group together. Usually these people came together to hold the hand of wives whose husbands were TDY in dangerous places, or who were alone because husbands were on extended isolated tours in the wilds of Korea or Alaska. Every Air Force Base had such a support net. They didn't usually meet to support an Air Force Master Sergeant whose husband had purposely lost himself in the desert, however.

Hushed conversations were going on all over. Amanda tried not to hear any of them. The whole situation was too much like a wake. *All that is missing is covered dishes and drinks,* she thought bitterly.

Different members of the support net took turns sitting or standing with Amanda in some sort of complicated rotation that she couldn't figure out. It didn't matter. She was glad they were there to hold her hand. *I'd be a hysterical wreck without them,* she thought.

The phone rang at 1215 and Amanda picked it up. The hushed talk fell quiet. It was Master Sergeant Holbrook from the Edwards Security Police.

"Sergeant Pentland, we just got a call from the CHP (California Highway Patrol.) They have found your car."

"They found the car," she announced to the room. "And my husband?"

"No. I'm sorry. Just the car."

Amanda drew in a shaking breath and clamped the lid

155

tighter on her emotions. She wanted to scream and weep and curse, but she didn't. "Where was the car?" she asked.

"A CHP plane spotted it. It was parked well off highway 14 up near Red Rock Canyon. Do you know where that is?"

"Yes."

"The keys were still in it and the driver's side door was standing open."

"But Daniel wasn't there."

"Right. CHP and the Kern county Sheriff's department are searching the area now. There are dogs on the way there. That'll help. They'll keep us updated. I gave them your number too. I take it they haven't called."

"No."

"Have you got a pencil? I'll give you the number for Search and Rescue."

"OK."

Holbrook reeled off the number and Amanda wrote it down. Holbrook paused a second then said, "Sergeant Pentland, you're not there alone are you? I can have someone out there to stay with you in just a couple of minutes."

"I'm not alone" she said. "I have several friends here from the chapel, but thank you for the thought sergeant."

"All right then. I wish I had more news for you. Better news," he said.

"Me too. But thanks all the same."

"They'll find him Sergeant Pentland," Holbrook said, but the sound of doubt was in his voice. It was 110 degrees and dry as mummy wrappings. A man could die of dehydration in less than 8 hours.

"Thank you again," Amanda said. She hung up the phone and tears slipped past her tight control. *Oh Danny please please don't be dead. Please,* she thought.

Mrs. Quinn noticed the tears and put her arms around Amanda. Amanda put her head against Mrs. Quinn's shoulder.

"He's looking for Kit out in the desert," Amanda said. "He used to fight for her in dreams and then he stopped dreaming. Now he's looking for her in the desert."

Mrs. Quinn didn't understand what Amanda was talking about, but it didn't matter. "They'll find him Amanda. They'll find him," she said.

***

Kit called her mother and told her what had happened. Daniel sat on the bed and watched. He could only hear Kit's half of the conversation, but he gathered that her mother was less than pleased with the outcome. "I'm all right Mum, it's just a twist fracture to my wrist. It's not even really broken exactly."

She listened for a time.

"No," she said. "David is still in hospital I think. From what the police said he was injured rather badly."

Again silence.

"Yes. Daniel did. It was frightening. I'm still almost sick to my stomach. I really thought David was dead—

"No I don't have a police record. I wasn't arrested and neither was Daniel— Nor David.

"I don't think David will bother me again, no."

She listened again for a long time, then said, "Mother! I told you before I love him. No! I will not... I don't know. As long as we can. A few more days at least... Mother, I will go back to Italy without coming home if you don't stop it," she threatened.

At last Kit said, "Yes. All right. I don't think he will, but if David shows up at the house call the police. Don't wait; don't talk to him or anything, just call the police. All right then. I know you do, and I love you too. Ta." She hung up but sat staring at the phone.

"I take it Mum was upset," Daniel said.

Kit laughed balefully. "That is an understatement if ever there was one. But can you blame her? I mean her only

157

daughter is detained by the police for being involved in a street brawl between her former lover and her current lover who just happens to be a married American old enough to be her father."

Every word was like a blow to Daniel. He almost wished she would hit him. He could have dealt with the physical pain. "Ah Christ Kit, I'm sorry. I'm sorry." he said and put his head in his hands.

She turned and saw him slumped and defeated looking. It made her realize what she had just said and how it must have had sounded to Daniel. She got up from the phone table and came to sit beside him. "You have nothing to be sorry about. You were protecting me. Thank you."

"Didn't do much of a job did I?" he said, and touched the cast on her wrist. "Does it still hurt?"

"It throbs a little. I need some aspirin. It will be all right."

Daniel got up, opened his back pack and pulled out a flat travel tin of Bayer Aspirin. He shook out three, ran a glass of water and handed them to her.

Kit looked at the three pills in her hand then at Daniel. "I don't understand you," she said. "I thought you were the kindest, most gentle man I had ever met, but you really wanted to kill David, didn't you? I saw it in your eyes. It frightened me."

He sat back down beside her on the bed. "I don't know," he said. "Maybe I really did. Maybe that was why I smashed his nose when I could see he was beaten. He hurt you. He hit you in the face and broke your wrist and... I don't know."

"And then you turned back into my Daniel," she said and took the aspirin.

"Doctor Jekyll and Mister Hyde. That's me."

She leaned against his shoulder and reached up to touch his face. "I'm sorry about what I said. I didn't mean it the way it sounded."

"It sounded like the truth and that was what hurt," he said

and kissed the top of her head.

The next three days were not like the exquisite dream of the previous days, but they had more depth. More weight. Kit and Daniel learned more about each other. They tasted of one another as of bottles of wine drunk to the dregs. And in the depth of learning Daniel decided what he must do.

"I'm going to tell Amanda, Kit. I'm going to ask her for a divorce."

Kit gazed at him a long time before she said, "Are you sure? I am willing to go on like this, forever if need be. Are you sure?"

"She has supported me in almost everything I ever did. Hell, she has been my meal ticket for twenty of the last thirty years while I scribbled on like some damn—" he shook his head. "But, I'm sure. I'll work in a coal mine or on a garbage truck to keep us alive if I have to. If I never write another word in my life. I'm sure."

Kit took his hand and kissed it. She knew Daniel meant what he said and it made her happy in one way, but it made her feel low and dirty too. "When will you tell her?" she asked.

"She's in Germany right now. I don't know when she will be back. I'm going to call home to see if she left a message on the machine about when she'll be back. If I don't find out anything," he paused and gnawed at his bottom lip for a moment. "I don't know what I'll do from there. Maybe call her office to find out where she is and go there. One way or another I'm going to tell her as soon as I can."

Friday morning Daniel called home. He listened to his own voice tell him about how to leave a message then pressed one and zero on the phone. The box beeped and made a whirring sound then began to playback. It went through the message he had left Amanda then to Colonel Preston's voice. "Dan, the time is 1321, Thursday the 18th. I don't know where you went in England. I called Mildenhall, but they didn't know either. I hope you get this message soon. Please call me ASAP day or night at the office or at home. Bye."

The message box gave the two beeps that meant there were no more messages then disconnected. Daniel was left staring at the dead receiver in his hand.

"What is it Daniel? You are white as a ghost." Kit said.

He hung up the receiver and, without answering her went to his pack and dug out his small address book. He went back to the phone and dialed Amanda's office.

Kit came and stood beside him. She asked again, "What's wrong?"

"I don't know yet," he said. "Something... Hello. This is Dan Pentland may I speak to Colonel Preston please."

Preston was on in a second. "Dan, where are you?"

"London. What's up?"

"God, I hate to tell you this over the phone—"

A thrill of dread went through Daniel. "Just tell me," he said.

Preston hesitated another moment then said, "There's been a plane crash. A C-130 went down in the Eiffel mountains yesterday..."

An unbidden rush of joy ran through Daniel. All on its own his mind said, *This will simplify things.* In the next instant he realized what he had thought and a sick feeling grabbed his stomach.

Preston was still talking. "...Amanda was manifested on that plane."

Daniel's legs went weak and he subsided into the chair beside the table.

"Are you still there, Dan?" Preston asked.

"Yes, I'm here. Can you get me an emergency lift to— Where, Spangdahlm?"

"Better you should come back here until we get some more of this sorted out. I'll call Mildenhall. Can you get there?"

"Yes. I'll leave now and be there within a couple of hours if the trains are right."

"I could send a car."

"That may be necessary, but let me check first. I'll call you back. Just get me a seat on the first thing out of Mildenhall."

"OK. " Preston paused a moment then said, "I'm sorry, Dan."

"Thank you, sir. I'll call you back in half an hour or so."

"OK. Goodbye.

"Goodbye," Daniel answered and dropped the phone back into its cradle.

"Daniel, what is it?" Kit asked.

"It's Amanda. She was in a plane crash..."

The unbidden welling of joy came up in Daniel's chest again followed by the clutch of sickness in his belly. He leapt from the chair and into the bathroom and vomited until he was weak and shaking and empty.

An hour and a half later Kit stood beside him on the King's Cross station platform. "I wish I could go with you," she said. "Will you be all right?"

"I'm OK," he said, but he didn't look it. He had thrown up until the muscles of his belly ached with the strain. He could barely hold water down. "I wish you could come too, but..." he stopped.

"I'm so sorry, Daniel," she said and put her arms around him. She could feel the tension thrumming through his body. "I love you," she said.

"Oh God, Kit. How could this happen? Why did this happen?" His thoughts were a chaotic jumble of things he needed to do mixed with the joy which seemed to come in waves followed by guilt and sickness.

"I'll have to call Jack and Mitch," he said. "God! Where are their phone numbers?" He began to swing his pack down off his shoulder to dig for the address book.

161

Kit squeezed him tighter and he stopped. "Don't think about it now. You can look up the numbers when you are on the train. Just let me hold you right now. You can think later. Just go through what you must go through and don't think."

He relaxed a little. "I'll call you at your Mum's house as soon as I know anything. Are you OK?"

"I'm fine. Don't worry about me. Take care of yourself."

The train conductor blew his whistle and Daniel tore himself away from Kit. "I love you," he said a last time and got on the train.

Kit watched the train pull away and bleak emptiness came upon her like a cold wind. *Be safe, my darling. I love you,* she thought, and then added a prayer. *Please God, give him the strength he needs to get through this.*

Daniel spent the train ride trying hard to do what Kit had said and not think, but his mind would not shut off. It was a jumble of memory and wish and guilt and joy. Thirty years he had known Amanda. Twenty eight years he had been married to her, and he had loved her for all of them. He loved her still for that matter. But then there was Kit. With Amanda dead he could marry Kit.

His belly clenched, but there was nothing more to bring up.

Why did you do this to me God? he thought. *Why couldn't you just leave me alone? Why did you have to bring Kit into my life? Why did you let Amanda die? Why? Why? Why?* But only an echoing universal silence answered him.

A female airman who looked twelve years old met him with a taxi at Ely station. "Mr. Pentland, we have a plane waiting," she said.

"For me?"

"Yes sir. There was a packet run going anyway so we delayed it a couple of hours. You should be in Aviano in three hours."

Preston out did himself, Daniel thought.

In forty five minutes Daniel was driving onto the tarmac beside an Air Force Lear Jet. There was another automobile parked there with its engine running. When the taxi pulled up a British customs official stepped out of the waiting car, took Daniel's passport, stamped it and said as he handed it back, "I'm very sorry for your loss sir." Fifty-five minutes after he stepped down from the train at Ely Station Daniel was airborne.

Three hours later the Lear Jet touched down at Aviano. Daniel, dizzy from the speed of everything that had happened, and sick with grief and guilt, dragged himself on wobbly legs through the arrival door of the Aviano terminal. His mind was turned inward, gripping itself to keep him from flying into a thousand emotional pieces.

"Danny!" a female voice said.

Daniel's head snapped up. There, standing just the other side of the customs gate, was Amanda. Suddenly Daniel couldn't breathe. The room spun and got fuzzy at the edges and he sat down hard on the floor.

Daniel came to lying on the terminal floor. There was a Senior Airman hunched over him waving smelling salts under his nose. It made Daniel cough and try to sit up.

"Whoa, hold it right there," the Senior Airman said holding Daniel down with a firm hand on his chest. "Just take it easy for a minute 'till the world quits spinning."

"Amanda?" Daniel said, wondering if she had been a hallucination.

"I'm here, baby," Amanda said and stepped into his range of view. She looked worried and beautiful. The senior airman stepped out of the way and Amanda knelt down beside him. She leaned in and kissed her husband.

"But they said a plane crash," Daniel said, still hardly able to breathe. "You were dead in a plane crash."

Amanda shook her head. "I was supposed to be on that plane, but they pulled me off at the last minute and stuck me on another plane to go to a Partnership for Peace meeting in Prague."

Colonel Preston stepped closer and looked over Amanda's shoulder. "They didn't take time to change the manifest," he said. "Amanda didn't even know the plane had gone down until she landed here a few minutes before you landed."

Daniel threw his arms around Amanda and hugged her so hard it made her joints crackle. "Oh God I thought you were dead. I thought I had lost you. I love you, I love you!" he said all in a rush of relief.

"I'm sorry about all this, Dan," Colonel Preston said. "I know this scared you to death."

Daniel looked at Preston and decided he truly hated the man. "I'm gonna try to sit up now," he said.

Amanda moved back and helped him lift himself up. He was still dizzy, but the room was much firmer than it had been a few moments ago. He took a few deep breaths and stood. "OK," he said. "I'm OK. Can we go home now?"

"I'll take you myself," Preston said.

"The car is parked over by your office," Daniel said.

"We'll get it later," Amanda said, holding onto Daniel's arm as if it were a lifeline.

Oh God! What am I gonna do now? he thought. For all his decision back in London, now, under the circumstances, he couldn't tell Amanda he wanted a divorce. She was just back from the dead! He had just told her he loved her and was glad she was not dead. He couldn't tell her about Kit now. Not now. Not this minute.

But Kit. He had to let her know what had happened. He looked at his watch. It was 5:00 PM. Kit would still be on the train heading for New Castle. *I can't get hold of her yet... I'll wait. I could leave a message with her mother... No. I'll wait. I'll wait to tell Amanda. I'll wait until tomorrow.*

XIII

Amanda was on the verge of screaming hysteria. The only reason she didn't actually slip over was because she didn't want to look like an idiot in front of all the people in the house. *That is probably why they have wakes after funerals,* she thought. *People don't want to appear crazy in front of friends so they hold together.* When she realized which way her thoughts were headed she shoved them away as hard as she could. *This is no wake,* she said to herself. *He's alive and they are going to find him. This is not a wake!*

Amanda had called Search and Rescue three times in the last four hours and they had told her nothing. They still had not found any trace of Daniel except the car. The wind was blowing hard and it had blown all tracks away from the car. Even the dogs were having a hard time because the wind raised the dust which ruined the dogs' sense of smell. She wanted to run out into the desert and begin looking for Daniel herself, though she knew that was stupid. *What could I do?* She thought. Go calling for him like you would call for a child lost in a supermarket? Search and Rescue were doing the best they could and she could only wait.

The sun was going down. It was still furnace hot, but in an hour the temperature would begin to drop. In two hours it would be 75 degrees and the rapid change could do as much harm to a human being as if the 75 were 35.

The telephone rang and Amanda was on it before it finished its first ring. Again all the conversations in the house fell silent.

"Mrs. Pentland?" a male voice asked.

"Yes."

"This is Deputy Bill Hayes, Kern County Search and

Rescue. We found your husband."

Amanda's breath almost stopped. "You found him?" she said but didn't go on to the next question.

"He had climbed up into a little cave we couldn't see. The dogs found him."

"Is he all right?"

"He's alive—"

"Thank God," she said. A sigh of relief went through the people in the house.

"–but he was very dehydrated and sunburned."

"Where is he? Where did you take him?"

"He was Helicopter Medi-vac-ed to Bakersfield Memorial about an hour ago."

"Bakersfield," she repeated for those listening. Her heart was singing with joy.

"They confirmed they had him just before I called you. The guys that found him started an IV almost the instant they found him." Amanda could hear the deputies' satisfied smile through the telephone. "I'm no doctor," he went on, "but I'd say he has a good chance."

"Thank you," Amanda said. "Thank you for all your help."

"You're entirely welcome Ma'am," Deputy Hayes said and hung up.

Amanda tried to hang up the phone but she couldn't see very well through the tears of relief that were running down her face.

Chaplain Quinn's wife was at her side in a moment and took the receiver from her and hung it up. She put her arms round Amanda and held her until she stopped shaking.

***

Early spring sun poured through the glass doors of the bedroom. The snow atop the Dolomite Alps reflected the light so well Amanda could hardly look at them. She loved this house. She loved being in bed beside her husband and looking out at the Alps, but that feeling was a little tempered somehow by the way Daniel was acting.

It was two days after she had "returned from the dead" as Daniel put it and they were sleeping in. The first night had been sweet. Daniel had been completely solicitous and wonderful except in one area. Amanda had made sexual overtures but he had rebuffed them. Gently and with pleas that he was totally exhausted, which Amanda could believe to be sure, but rebuffed all the same. They ended with Daniel turned spoon wise against her back with his arm over her. It was deliciously warm and comforting, but something was missing. It was the same as before she left only more so.

Several times the following day she had caught Daniel staring at her as though he were on the verge of saying something, but when she asked what it was he only shook his head. "Just glad you are alive again," he said.

"Not Again, I was never anything but alive."

"Not to me. Until I set eyes on you in the terminal you were dead, and then you were alive again."

Amanda laughed, but there seemed to be more significance to it in his mind than she was allowing.

Now he lay beside her in the sun drenched room and slept. Truly slept. She knew he had been having trouble sleeping before she left and had been pretending to sleep sometimes, but this was real. The soft rasp of his breathing told her so. She had been listening to that not quite snore for almost thirty years.

Amanda sat up and studied Daniel's sleeping form. He was no movie star in the looks department, but there was a masculinity about him that still made her tingle when she thought about it. His gray streaked hair gave him a distinguished look that Amanda liked. His face was peaceful but, with a memory of trouble on it. The lines on his forehead seemed deeper and there was tension in his jaw line even when he was asleep. *I wonder why?* she thought, but put the thought aside. He had always been hard to read. There were worlds inside him that she had never fathomed and she had stopped trying long ago. She simply loved him and endured his moods.

Amanda suddenly smiled. She had a wickedly wonderful idea. She would ambush him while he was asleep.

She slid back down under the covers and scooted against him as much as she could. He was on his side facing her with knees pulled up slightly, but she pressed herself against him and his legs straightened in reaction. She put her arm over him and softly kissed his lips.

Daniel stirred and mumbled "Kit?"

The name was like a jolt of electricity. She jumped away from him as though she had been shocked.

Daniel was only half awake now, not sure what was happening. Amanda, in her cotton nightgown was sitting up beside him with a look of horror on her face.

"What is it?" Daniel asked. "What's wrong?"

Amanda was breathing hard, caught between tears of rage and tears of hurt. "You called me Kit," she said. Her voice sounded choked. "I kissed you and you called me Kit!"

Daniel blinked and opened his mouth, but no words came out.

"You've been sleeping with that English bitch haven't you?" she accused. "That's why you haven't wanted me."

"Amanda..."

"That's why you were in England wasn't it? You were holed up with her."

Daniel dropped his head.

"You bastard!" she said with growing intensity.

"Yes," he said.

"You bastard! You Bastard! You BASTARD!" she screamed and swung her fist around. It hit him hard on the left side of the face.

Daniel jerked with the force of the blow, but he made no attempt to protect himself.

Sometimes in Dreams

Amanda, in full fury hit him again and again in the face screeching like a panther. Daniel sat and endured, never as much as raising his hands to ward off the blows.

When her fury cooled enough to let her stop hitting him she sat panting with the exertion and staring at her husband. "It's over," she said between heavy breaths. "No more! You'll never see her again at all. You understand!"

Daniel looked up. "No," he said and shook his head. "It isn't over. Nothing is over. I love Kit. I love her. We tried to make it not be so. We tried. But we couldn't stop it. I love her."

Her husband's words, softly but firmly said, hit Amanda harder than any blow he could have landed. They crushed all the fury in her and left her empty.

"Amanda, I want you to know that I love you..." Daniel said.

The words were so incongruous they made Amanda laugh. "You love me?" she said and raised her hand to hit him again, but didn't. "You're fucking that English whore, but you love me?" She said again with utter disbelief.

"...and I hate hurting you like this," he finished.

"But you're willing to for that tight little cunt..."

"Don't call her that" he raised his voice for the first time, shouting Amanda down.

"She is not some whore off the street, Amanda. She is kind and loving and sweet and she did not want this to hurt you. She begged me not to tell you but—"

"She wanted your little trysts to go on without any commitment! Just like a whore!"

"I am going to marry her as soon as I can get a divorce from you!"

Amanda's mouth fell open. "You're not serious?" She said. "There's no way that is going to happen."

"It will. I'm going to go to her one way or another. My heart is already there. I'm sorry, but that is what is going to happen."

Amanda shook her head. "No. I'll see you both dead first," she said. "You'll never live with her. You'll never see her again. You'll never leave me. I won't let you!"

The front door bell rang. Daniel and Amanda stared at one another and didn't move. They were suddenly embarrassed with their flaming emotional melodrama, as if caught naked in the middle of a street.

It rang again.

Amanda saw a light of hope click on in Daniel's eyes and knew what it meant.

It couldn't be, Daniel thought, but his heart wouldn't let the hope go. *Kit, Kit, Kit!*

His mind chanted. Despite all that had happened, despite the hurt and pain of a second before his heart soared.

It was as though Amanda could read his mind and the fury that had exploded a moment before exploded again. She flew out of bed and ran down the hall to the front door wearing nothing but her nightgown.

Daniel took a step toward the door then remembered that he was naked and grabbed a robe. He stepped into the hall just as Amanda threw open the door to find Canon Doyle standing on the porch with his hat in his hand. A taxi sat on the street with its engine running.

"Father Doyle. What are you doing here?" Amanda asked.

Daniel came up behind her, but did not touch her.

Father Doyle glanced from Amanda's face up to Daniel's. He frowned in confusion. The blows Amanda had landed were starting to bruise and swell.

"Daniel," the priest began as though not quite in phase with the world. He paused and looked at Amanda then went on. "Daniel, it's Kit Marlowe."

"Kit? What about her?" Daniel said, elbowing past Amanda.

Doyle hesitated. He seemed as though he were about to weep. "Her mother called me this morning. She would have called you, but she didn't have the number."

"What? Why? Why didn't she just get it from Kit?"

"Daniel," the priest said. "Kit died last night."

Daniel shook his head. He knew he had heard wrong. Kit was in New Castle, and she was going to be back in Venice in a few days. She was... "What?" he said.

"What did you say?" Amanda asked.

"Kit is dead, Daniel," Doyle repeated. "A man named David Albee shot her in front of her mother's house in New Castle then turned the gun on himself." Tears began trickling from the priest's eyes and his voice choked. After a moment he cleared his throat and said, "This Albee was a jilted lover or something."

***

Amanda tried to stop Daniel from going to Kit's funeral, not because of the affair, but because she could see how close to the edge of madness he was; but it was useless. With or without her he would have gone to New Castle. At last she relented and went with her beloved to New Castle to bury his beloved. As they traveled he told her the whole story of London and the fight, and through it all he kept returning to," I should have killed him. I almost did. I should have finished the job. Kit would be alive if I had just killed him." It was all told in a voice as flat and emotionless as gray iron chains. He did not weep, he did not curse, he did not sleep. So far as Amanda knew he did not sleep even after Kit was safely buried and they had returned to Aviano. There, still unable to sleep, Daniel was prescribed some sleeping pills. The morning after he had gotten them, in the sunny house in Marsure while Amanda was at work, he swallowed the whole bottle, washing it down with a quart of milk. If Amanda had not come home for lunch he would have died.

The remainder of the Aviano assignment was curtailed on

humanitarian grounds. Colonel Preston, Amanda's boss, had a great deal to do with the curtailment. She could never quite understand why he had worked so hard for her then since he had always been a demanding pain in the ass before.

The Pentlands returned to their home of record which was California. Amanda had served almost twenty years. She would finish the assignment to Edwards and retire with twenty three years of active Air Force Service.

***

Chaplain Quinn and his wife drove Amanda to Bakersfield Memorial Hospital. It was a silent drive in the thickening evening dark. Almost two hours and not more than twenty words were said. Amanda was closed tight into herself. She was caught between joy and despair; so glad that Daniel was alive she could have danced all the way to the hospital, but so heartbroken that this man whom she had loved for so long had wanted so much to leave her that he had tried again to die.

Daniel was in a room that would have held two other patients, but he was alone. When Amanda came to the door she stopped and looked in. The room was dark except for a small standing light near the bed. Chaplain and Mrs. Quinn were with her. When she stopped at the door the Chaplain asked, "Are you all right? Do you want to wait a little while? He looks like he is sleeping comfortably. You can wait a little while if you want."

Amanda shook her head. "I'm all right. Would you please give me a few minutes alone with him before you come in?"

Quinn nodded. "Sure. We'll go wait down the hall. Just holler if you need us."

"Thank you—for everything," Amanda said.

The other two nodded and turned away

Daniel had been a large vigorous man once, but now looked shrunken and old. His hair, once dark and streaked with gray was almost all gray now. His face was blotches of pale gray and angry red. The sun had blistered him until he was almost unrecognizable. An IV bag hung on the rack beside the bed dripping life giving fluids into his dehydrated body.

Amanda took a deep breath and stepped into the room. She didn't say anything, but walked as quietly as she could to a chair that was beside the bed and sat down. Her hands wanted to reach out and touch Daniel, but she didn't want to wake him. *It has been so long since he slept,* she thought.

A half hour passed. Amanda watched the IV drip and Daniel's chest rise and fall. He was alive, but he was a shell. *Dear God what am I going to do?* she prayed.

Daniel groaned and thrashed feebly. Amanda reached out and touched his arm. "It's OK Baby," she said. "It's all right. I'm here. It's all right."

"'Manda?" Daniel asked. His voice was dry and cracked.

"Hi Danny."

"M thirsty. Drink of water?"

There was a plastic water pitcher and glass sitting beside the bed. She poured a glass and put a bent plastic straw into it, then held it while he drank.

"Thank you," he said.

Amanda put the glass back on the table and sat down again.

"I saw her 'Manda," he said.

A chill went through Amanda. "Who?" she asked though she knew very well who.

"Kit. I saw Kit. She has been calling me for a long time and I saw her."

"No Danny, you didn't. It was just the heat and the thirst. She died two years ago. You didn't see her."

"I know she died 'Manda. But I saw her. She came to me when I was laying there. She knelt down beside me and touched my face."

Amanda began to cry softly.

"No 'Manda, don't. Don't cry. I love you. Don't cry."

"Danny you don't love me. You ran off into the desert to

173

get away from me. You ran off looking for a girl that has been dead two years."

"She told me to live 'Manda. She knelt down beside me and told me to love you and live."

Amanda wiped her eyes with the back of her hand and gazed into Daniel's eyes for a long time. They didn't seem fevered or crazy no matter how he sounded.

"And are you going to live Danny?" She asked.

"If you want me to."

She looked at her husband a long time before she said, "I want you to."

Daniel smiled. It was almost like the old Daniel except for the cracked and sunburned lips. "I'm tired 'Manda," he said. "I'm gonna take a nap now. OK?"

"Sure Danny. It's OK. Go ahead and sleep. I'll stay right here."

He smiled again and closed his eyes. In moments his breathing was slow and regular. It stayed that way all night.

THE END

Sometimes in Dreams

About G.L HELM

G. Lloyd Helm is a 'ne'er-do-well scribbler'—novelist, short story writer and poet—who has tramped around the world for the last forty years thanks to his long suffering military wife. He has lived in Germany, Spain, and Italy. His epitaph will read, "He married well."

21105835R00100

Made in the USA
Charleston, SC
06 August 2013